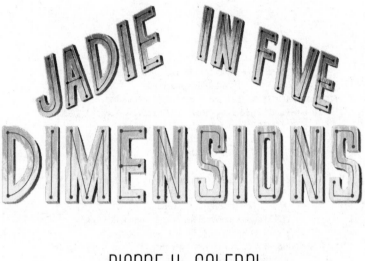

JADIE IN FIVE DIMENSIONS

DIANNE K. SALERNI

HOLIDAY HOUSE ⬩ NEW YORK

HOLIDAY HOUSE is registered in the U.S. Patent and Trademark Office.
Printed and bound in May 2021 at Maple Press, York, PA, USA.
www.holidayhouse.com
First Edition
1 3 5 7 9 10 8 6 4 2

Library of Congress Cataloging-in-Publication Data

Names: Salerni, Dianne K., author.
Title: Jadie in five dimensions / Dianne K. Salerni.
Other titles: Jadie in 5 dimensions
Description: First edition. | New York City : Holiday House, [2021]
Audience: Ages 9–12. | Audience: Grades 4–6.
Summary: Thirteen-year-old Jadie lives in 4-space and works as an
Agent for the four-dimensional beings who adopted her after
being abandoned as an infant, but when Jadie learns her
origin story is a lie she works to uncover the truth.
Identifiers: LCCN 2020039134 | ISBN 9780823449095 (hardcover)
Subjects: CYAC: Space and time—Fiction. | Families—Fiction
Kidnapping—Fiction. | Science fiction.
Classification: LCC PZ7.S152114 Jad 2021 | DDC [Fic]—dc23
LC record available at https://lccn.loc.gov/2020039134

ISBN: 978-0-8234-4909-5 (hardcover)

For my nieces and nephews:
Abby and her three daughters; Stevie;
Cameron; Olivia; Joe; Evie; Dominic;
and in memory of Luke

DIMENSIONAL SPACE	DIRECTIONS TO MOVE
1-space	Forward, backward
2-space	Forward, backward, left, right
3-space	Forward, backward, left, right, up, down
4-space	Forward, backward, left, right, up, down, ana, kata
5-space	Forward, backward, left, right, up, down, ana, kata, and ??

1. JADIE

My target holds her phone against her ear, scurrying down the sidewalk in high heels. She's dragging a wheeled suitcase and carrying a tapestry bag over her shoulder. The bag has sunflowers on it, which is how I know I've got the right lady.

Coasting behind her on my skateboard, I weave between pedestrians. One man snarls at me—"Watch it, girl!"—even though I didn't touch him.

Great. Last thing I need is someone drawing attention to me.

Luckily, the woman is too busy talking on her phone to notice. She's heading for a subway entrance a block ahead, so I have to make my move.

A lot of kids on my middle school soccer team talk about getting into "the zone." I call it *Jadie 2.0*—an alternate me that pushes the regular Jadie Martin aside and tells my body what to do. *Speed up. Bend your knees. Lean left.*

Bearing down on the woman, I hook my fingers under the strap of her tapestry bag and hurl it as far as I can into traffic. The bag strikes the windshield of a taxi, spewing its contents over the car and into the street.

The woman whirls toward me with a furious shriek, her hands curved into manicured claws. Cutting sharply away on my board, I call over my shoulder, "Sorry!"

I only did what I was ordered to do.

Other people shout after me, but only the guy who yelled at me a few seconds ago gives chase. "Come back here, you little punk!"

I steer into the closest alley, which turns out to be a mistake. A delivery van blocks the exit, and two guys are stacking crates around the vehicle. There's no way I can get through them with the angry man ten steps behind me.

What I do next is against protocol, but I don't see an alternative. Hopping off the skateboard, I stamp on the back end and grab the front axle. As my pursuer barrels toward me, his hand outstretched, I stab the round button on my metal bracelet and vanish.

Or at least that's what it looks like to the man in the alley.

For me, it's like being knocked from my skateboard while traveling at top speed—a sudden wrench in a new direction. Not a normal direction like up, down, left, or right. I'm flying *kata,* out of three-dimensional space.

Shutting my eyes to keep from getting dizzy, I hold out my arm. Only when my feet hit a metal platform and my bracelet clicks into a port-lock do I blink and look around. The alley is gone, replaced by what looks like a modern art painting sprung to life. In front of me, gold loops squirm and blue orbs pulse. Off to my right, silver tubes intersect in impossible ways like an optical illusion—but this isn't an illusion.

This is 4-space.

I glance down between my feet, through the metal grid of the platform. Earth isn't visible to human eyes from this position, but it's there. My planet, the solar system, the Milky Way Galaxy . . . the entire three-dimensional universe, in fact, is nested inside the vastness of this four-dimensional universe the way one Russian doll fits inside another.

A red glow illuminates the space around me—bright enough to see by, but not as satisfying as sunlight or even a strong lightbulb. It reminds me of a fire burning in the wilderness, which always makes me wonder if these platforms are inside or outside. Or if *inside* and *outside* aren't the only two options when you have four spatial dimensions.

The only things that make sense to my eyes are the platform I'm standing on and the items I brought with me: my skateboard and my bracelet, where today's assignment is spelled out on a small screen.

Woman with luggage walking toward subway station. Sunflower tapestry bag. Throw into traffic.

Underneath these instructions are the spatial coordinates of the event—a string of numbers that mean nothing to me. They placed me in the correct location for my mission, but they aren't necessary to get me home.

At the edge of the platform there's a clunky console that looks like something from the 1960s. It has large numbered keys for entering coordinates on the way to a course correction, and three buttons labeled Complete, Incomplete, and Return to be used afterward.

Hugging my skateboard under my arm, I push Complete. The screen on my bracelet goes blank.

Assignments like this leave me conflicted. On one hand, I'm pumped with adrenaline, like when I intercept a ball on the soccer field. On the other hand, what I did was an aggressive act against a player unaware of the game.

It feels like a foul.

I hope things turn out okay for that lady. Maybe she would've been flattened by a bus at the next intersection and the delay I created saved her life. Or maybe, when she misses her train, she passes the time before the next one by buying a winning lottery ticket.

But Miss Rose tells us that the desired outcome of our missions rarely involves the target. The end result of throwing a purse into the street might be four steps removed from the act. Maybe the taxi that got hit with the bag misses a fare, and because of *that,* two people meet who wouldn't have met if the taxi had been there. They fall in love, get married, and have a kid who someday cures cancer.

That would make throwing a stranger's bag into traffic totally worthwhile.

After I've registered my assignment as complete, I push the Return button. The platform whirs into action, sliding past four identical but unoccupied platforms. Traveling through 4-space creates a shortcut between any two locations in 3-space. Therefore, it's only seconds before my platform stops, the port-lock releases my bracelet, and I'm yanked ana, the direction opposite from kata. The machine returns me to the same location I departed from earlier today: my bedroom in my house in Kansas, slipping me between the walls and the roof through the open fourth dimension (which is visible from 4-space even though humans can't perceive it). The adult Agents nicknamed this machine the Transporter because when it deposits me on the fuzzy blue rug in the center of my room, I appear in the blink of an eye, like in *Star Trek.*

Alia Malik looks up without any surprise and says, "Hey, Jadie." She's lying on my bed, scrolling on her phone. "Where you been?"

"A city. Not sure where." I drop my skateboard and nudge it with my foot, sending it off to a corner of the room. Alia isn't surprised that I appeared out of nowhere, but I'm a little surprised to see her. She's my neighbor and a fellow Agent, but she's not usually waiting in my bedroom when I get back from missions.

"I went to Thailand," she says. "Third time this month."

Alia, her sister, and her parents often get sent to Thailand, the country of Alia's grandparents. I wish I would get assignments overseas. "Did you see anything interesting?"

Alia snorts. "I was in a field. I opened a fence. What'd you do?"

"I threw some lady's purse into traffic."

"Jadie!" Alia gasps in partly fake, partly real horror. "You get all the mean ones."

She's not wrong. I hope it's because I'm athletic and not because Miss Rose thinks I'm a criminal at heart.

Alia flashes a wide, forced smile. "I have a favor to ask. Any chance you'd babysit for me tomorrow?" She holds up her arm and rattles a bracelet identical to mine.

Babysit. She wants me to take her bracelet and cover her assignments, which is against the rules. Course corrections are designed specifically for each Agent. We aren't supposed to swap them.

Alia sees my hesitation and starts begging. "Please, Jadie! There's a *Cosmic Knight* tournament tomorrow. I can't leave in the middle without forfeiting." Alia is obsessed with the online game *Cosmic Knight,* a race-slash-battle among alien players—water-breathing assassins, murderous spider ladies, poisonous floating gas bags—seeking a mysterious token that will protect the finder's homeworld from destruction. I played once, but I prefer soccer.

"If you tell Miss Rose, she won't give you a mission while it's going on," I point out. Our 4-space liaison doesn't assign course corrections during activities where our disappearance would be noticed. When Alia chews her fingernail and avoids my eyes, I get it. "Ohhh. You're grounded again."

She grimaces. "I failed a history test. I'm not supposed to be out of the house this weekend, except for course corrections, and Mom says no online activities for two weeks. But she and Dad will be at Tehereh's color guard competition tomorrow, soooo . . ."

"I have a soccer game in the morning."

"I wouldn't need you until one o'clock."

I sigh.

"I already asked Huan and Jin." Those are the fifteen-year-old Agents across the cul-de-sac. "But they're visiting colleges this weekend. I know your brother would do it—and

Ty probably would, *for a price*—but I don't trust them to get the job done. No offense to Marius."

"None taken." My brother, Marius, is always willing to help a friend but sometimes lacks good judgment. As for my next-door neighbor, Ty Rivers, I wouldn't want to give him that kind of blackmail material if I were Alia.

She presses her hands together. *"Help* me, Jadie Martin. You're my only hope."

I recognize the line from *Star Wars* but shoot back, "You mean your *last* hope. 'Cause you already asked Huan and Jin, crossed off Marius and Ty, and you can't ask your sister or one of the adults to do it."

"C'mon. I probably won't get an assignment during the couple of hours you have the bracelet." She hesitates. "I know you don't want to get in trouble with the Seers because of . . . you know . . . but—"

"Because of what?"

Alia shrugs like she doesn't want to bring it up. "Because you owe them your life."

My shoulders hunch automatically, but I try to look like it's no big deal.

Twelve years ago, my natural-born parents abandoned me by the side of a highway in the middle of a snowstorm. Like trash.

I should have died. But superintelligent beings from a higher dimension sent their best Agents to rescue me and raise me as their own daughter. I grew up in a loving family with great parents and a brother who's an idiot sometimes, but still my brother. For the past six months, since I turned thirteen, I've had the honor of serving as an Agent myself, assisting the Seers in their mission to put Earth on track for a brighter future. When they tell me to mug a lady on the street, I do it and do it well.

I see that Alia's face is falling, and I *feel* like trash on the side of the highway, disappointing my friend rather than break one tiny rule. It's only a couple of hours, and if Alia is asked to close a fence in Thailand, I can close that fence as well as she can. In fact, I bet I can close a fence like it's never been closed before.

"I'll do it."

2. SAM

Sam Lowell hears the apartment door open and close, but, engrossed in gluing Popsicle sticks together, he doesn't register it for several minutes.

The drawing in front of him serves as his guide. The "impossible cube," the geometric basis for the M. C. Escher print *Belvedere*, is simple to sketch—a cube with one of the back edges cleverly drawn to look like a front edge.

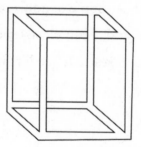

Of course, it's not really a cube but a two-dimensional drawing the human eye *imagines* as a cube. This object couldn't exist in three dimensions, although Sam has read it's possible to make parts of it from Popsicle sticks and—by photographing them from the right angle—cause them to *look* like an impossible cube.

It's trick photography, but it might help him with his project.

First, he has to get his fake cube parts assembled correctly. As he works, a series of thoughts penetrates the fortress of his concentration.

- One of his parents came home a few minutes ago.
- Dad is out of town, presenting his latest physics theory at Princeton and hoping for funding, a teaching position, or ideally, both.
- Mom had a job interview today. If things went well, she would've burst into Sam's room to tell him.

Sam puts down the sticks and the Elmer's glue. Spurning the crutch that leans against the wall, he pushes himself to his feet, careful not to put too much weight on his left leg. That knee has a tendency to give way without warning. The crutch helps, but he hates it.

There's an eerie, horror-movie, *what-am-I-going-to-find* feeling to those dozen steps down the hall that end at the sight of his mother seated on the living room couch, bent forward with her head in her hands. Cleopatra, their sleek black cat, rubs against her shins as if trying to provide comfort. Or asking to be fed.

"Mom?"

Her head jerks up, and for a second she tries to smile. Then her face crumples and tears come. "I didn't get it."

That, he'd already guessed. He looks at the time. It's six o'clock—later than he realized. "Were they interviewing you all this time just to tell you *no?*"

She shakes her head. "The woman was late. Missed her plane in Cincinnati. They said I could wait, that she was getting on the next flight. I sat there for two hours. When she finally showed up, she told me she filled the job *on the plane,* gave it away to the woman sitting next to her. She laughed like I was supposed to think it was funny—some kid tried to steal her bag and made her miss her first flight so that she ended up sitting next to a friend from college who needed a job." She throws out her hands. "What was I supposed to say? I needed that job!"

Sam plops down beside her on the couch and catches one of her hands in his own. "You should've told her off, Mom."

"I couldn't. You can't burn bridges."

Sam looks at their hands together. Her fingers are white and too thin, with nails bitten down to the nub. She slips her hand away from his and shifts it to his damaged knee. "How's the physical therapy?"

Sam hasn't been to therapy in weeks. The owner of the place, the guy who worked with Sam, was okay. But his wife ran the front desk and reminded Sam every visit how much money they owed. She kept saying, "Therapy can't take the place of reconstructive surgery. Has that been scheduled?" She knew perfectly well his parents didn't have insurance or any way to pay for surgery.

Cleo jumps onto the sofa beside him and butts her head against his hand. Sam rubs her ears and says, "They gave me exercises to work on at home."

His mother gazes at his face, and for a second Sam thinks she's going tell him he's not allowed to quit therapy. But her eyes are distant. "I have to call your father and tell him I didn't get the job."

Sam's good leg jiggles up and down. "You don't have to call him tonight. Let him—" *Let him present his proposal without worrying about you.* But he can't say that.

"He knew I had this interview. He's probably waiting to hear from me." She stands and picks up her phone while Sam watches, rubbing his hands against his jeans legs. Her eyes dart to the Lowell family portrait hanging on the wall above the bookshelves.

"We have more bad luck," she whispers, "than any family ought to have."

After she leaves the room to make the dreaded call in private, Sam stares at the photograph that's been haunting him practically his whole life. He doesn't want to feed Mom's paranoid delusions, but he has to admit it sometimes seems like the universe holds a grudge against the Lowell family.

With a sigh, he gets up to verify the number of pills his mother has left in her prescription and prepare himself for the battle of getting her to take them.

3. JADIE

My team massacres our opponents on Saturday morning, and Coach invites everyone to her house on Sunday for a make-your-own taco celebration. During the ride home, Mom and I verbally replay every high point of the game, and my good mood lasts until we pull into our neighborhood and I remember my promise to Alia.

It's not that I'm such a goody-two-shoes about breaking one small rule. And it's not because I think I owe the Seers. Alia's wrong about that. My life isn't a debt that needs to be paid. It's an *obligation*. The Seers didn't just *save* me; they chose to have me raised by Agents and trained as one myself. They have a purpose for me, and I don't want to let them down.

Mom drops me off and turns the car around for a grocery run. I shower and change, and then, even though I'm starving, I head for Alia's house because it's almost one o'clock.

The four houses in our cul-de-sac belong to the families who make up Miss Rose's Agents—ours first, then the Riverses, the Li house, and the Maliks. Miss Rose arranged it this way so we can avoid nosy neighbors and support each other while executing our duties.

Switching bracelets is probably not what she had in mind.

Outside, my brother and Ty are playing basketball in our driveway. Well, *Marius* is playing while Ty, who's about as athletic as belly button lint, stands to the side, hunched over his phone. "I'm telling you, it'll work," he says to Marius, tossing blond hair out of his eyes. "I'm positive."

Eyes on the net, Marius ignores his friend. Which, in my opinion, is a good thing because whatever Ty is planning will get Marius into trouble.

When they were eleven, they tried to blow up a tree stump with fireworks. Marius got his eyebrows singed off. When they were twelve, they used Ty's drone to strafe Melissa Pierce's birthday party with VOTE MARIUS CLASS PREZ campaign flyers. He lost all the girls' votes.

"Marius," Ty says loudly, trying to get his attention.

"In a minute." Marius nails a jump shot. "And the crowd goes wild!" He catches the ball on its bounce and struts in a circle, pumping his arm.

"Hey, give it here!" I shout, holding out my hands.

My brother grins and passes the ball to me. I catch it, dart around him, and execute a perfect lay-up. The ball drops through the hoop, and Marius intercepts it. "Niiice. But not as good as mine. One-on-one?" He waggles his eyebrows.

Ty glares balefully at me from beneath his bangs. I'm

tempted to say yes to thwart his latest caper, whatever it is. Plus, Marius and I have an ongoing friendly competition over sports, control of the television remote, and who finishes off the best leftovers in the refrigerator.

We're the same age, we think. He came to us when he was about three years old, speaking Spanish. Dad was assigned to rescue him from a burning building during a course correction and then, to the surprise and delight of my parents, was instructed to keep him and raise him in our family.

"Maybe later," I offer. "I promised to do something for Alia."

"Chicken." He only pretends to say it under his breath.

"You'll pay for that!"

When I knock on Alia's front door, she greets me wearing a headset and talking into a mic. "RL, dudes," she says. "AFK, BRB."

"LMNOP," I joke.

Alia doesn't laugh. I was hoping she'd tell me she already had a course correction today and doesn't need my help. Instead, she shoves the bracelet at me, mouths the word *Thanks*, and shuts the door in my face.

So. Much. Gratitude.

I head home, stuffing Alia's bracelet into my back pocket so Marius and Ty don't see it. I needn't have bothered. They're both gone from the cul-de-sac when I walk through, and from the silence in our house, I assume they've gone to Ty's.

Lunch pickings are slim, which is why Mom went to the store, so I heat a frozen burrito. When my back pocket starts beeping, I mistake it at first for the microwave before fumbling Alia's bracelet out.

The screen says:

Laptop on desk beside glass of water. Spill water. Blame the cat.

This seems pretty fail-proof. I wait for the burrito to finish heating and gobble it down because I'm not leaving for any mission, simple or not, on an empty stomach. With a belch, I jog upstairs to my bedroom to depart from my usual launch point.

Since the Transporter always returns you to the precise point you came from, everyone in my family has a designated location for departure. Otherwise, you might land on an unsuspecting family member on your way back into 3-space!

Inside my room, I unsnap my bracelet, lay it on my dresser, and slip Alia's on. It's loose around my wrist, but not enough to slide off. Standing on my fuzzy blue rug, I tighten the ponytail at the back of my head and then push the call button.

When I feel the tug of the Transporter, I close my eyes and let it yank me out of my universe.

Two seconds later, the bracelet hits a port-lock but doesn't seem to catch. My eyes fly open as my chest hits the console *hard,* and I grab on with my free arm. Making sure both feet are square in the middle of the platform, I check the port-lock, but it's securely latched after all. The landing felt different because Alia's bracelet fits loosely.

I exhale in relief. Falling into 4-space is not something any Agent wants to do. Miss Rose often refers to Earth as a membrane world—or sometimes *braneworld*—because 4-space is so immense the entirety of our universe fits inside it like a scrap of tissue. In spite of this, traveling by Transporter is supposed to be absolutely safe—otherwise my parents wouldn't allow me and Marius to do it. I'm more likely to encounter something hazardous on Earth than here in the fourth dimension.

At this moment, however—on an unauthorized mission—I don't exactly feel protected.

"Chill out," I mutter. Releasing my death grip on the console, I punch in the coordinate numbers from the bracelet screen. The platform shifts through 4-space, the port-lock clicks open, and I'm dropped ana, back to Earth.

I land in a bedroom—a small, cramped room where the bed and desk and dresser are so close together there's barely room to walk between them. My arrival startles a black cat that was sleeping on the bed. It leaps to the floor and bolts from the room, the bell on its collar jingling.

Judging by the decorations and the clothes sticking out of overstuffed drawers, this is a boy's room. There are lots of books, especially textbooks. A crutch leans against one wall, and a laptop sits, as promised, on the desk next to a glass of water. Hanging on the wall above it is an M. C. Escher print that Miss Rose once used in a lesson on four dimensions.

The instructions say I'm supposed to blame the cat. So I better catch the cat and shut it in this room before completing my mission.

The Seers probably planned this mission for a time when the residence is empty, but it doesn't hurt to be cautious. I tiptoe down the hall of what appears to be an apartment, approaching the entrance to a living room. When I hear nothing—no voices, no TV—I call softly, "Here, kitty, kitty."

The cat meows from the top of a waist-high set of bookshelves.

"Good kitty." I approach slowly, wondering how to pick it up without getting scratched or bitten. But when I reach out, the cat trills happily and climbs into my arms. "Well, you're friendly, aren't you?"

He—no, *she* butts her head against my chin. Scratching her

ears, I glance up at a framed family photograph hanging on the wall. It's one of those formal portraits you can get taken at the mall, the mom and dad seated on chairs in front of a fake backdrop with their kids on their laps.

The boy, dressed in a little blue suit with a tie, looks like he's about three years old.

The girl is only a baby, sitting on her mom's lap in a sleeveless pink dress. The beige skin of her left arm is marked by a stark white birthmark that stretches across her elbow and halfway down her forearm.

My heart flops over in my chest. I drop the cat.

4. JADIE

Wrenching my eyes away from the photograph, I look at the patch of whitish skin that stretches across my elbow and down my forearm. All my life I've had to tell people: *No, I don't have paint on my arm—no, it's not a burn or a scar—and no, it's not a contagious rash.*

I run my fingers over the birthmark even though there's nothing to *feel*. Doctors say it's just faulty skin pigmentation, but I need the touch of my fingertips running along its outline to verify what my eyes are telling me. The birthmark on the baby in the photo is the same shape and in the same place as mine.

I search the picture for other similarities. Her eyes are light brown, like mine. Her hair is kinky-curly and a variegated golden brown that my dad calls caramel popcorn. And by dad, I mean *Dad*, not—

My gaze shifts from the little girl to the father and the mother. Could these be the depraved people who abandoned a baby by the side of a highway in the dead of winter? Why'd they set up a picture shrine for her, then? There are four framed pictures of this baby girl on top of the bookshelves.

"It *can't* be me!" I whisper, grabbing the photos one by one to examine them.

When the pain in my chest becomes unbearable, I realize I've been holding my breath. Slamming one of the pictures down on the shelf, I exhale and suck in air. *C'mon, Jadie. What's Coach always telling you? Breathe, think, and then act. Play smart.*

Taking deep, slow breaths, I look around and focus on details. There are pictures of the little boy too—all around the room. But the boy grows older. There are school pictures and Boy Scout pictures and one where he's holding an award.

There are only baby pictures of the little girl.

And an album.

Silently, I thank my coach for her advice; otherwise I might not have noticed the vinyl book lying on top of the bookshelves, in a place of honor right beneath that family photograph. I fumble open the cover.

For my daughter, Jocelyn Dakota Lowell.

The name is written in flowing script beneath a picture of a newborn in a hospital crib, along with a date that's very near the one my parents picked to celebrate my birthday.

My shaking hand turns the page. More photos: mother and baby in a hospital bed . . . father holding the baby . . . toddler brother standing on a chair to peer into a hospital crib . . .

There are captions in that same script: *Big brother Sam takes his first look at you.*

I'm about to turn another page, when—voices.

I stare at the front door like it's something out of a scary movie. Voices getting nearer. Footsteps. Me standing here, frozen in place.

Alia's course correction should have taken mere seconds. The Seers didn't plan for an Agent to be here longer than that.

The *all-knowing* Seers who said I'd been an abandoned baby.

Saved by their mercy and wisdom.

Alia's bracelet has the location code at the bottom of the screen, though I have no idea where I am. The United States, probably, but where?

Outside the apartment, keys jingle as if someone is searching for the right one.

Just like when there's thirty seconds left in a game and I *have* to score, Jadie 2.0 takes over. My every movement is purposeful and efficient. Tucking the baby album under one arm, I stride across the room and pick up a pen from the coffee table while the bolt on the front door turns. I hit the button on my bracelet at the exact moment the door opens.

The apartment blurs as I soar kata, and I tighten my grip on the album. I've brought my skateboard on course corrections many times—and once a lacrosse stick—but never have I held on to anything as desperately as this book.

When I reach the Transporter platform, I balance the album on the console, nudge the cover open, and use the pen to copy the numbers from the bracelet onto the first page. I check twice to make sure I have the sequence correct. *451. 622. 8407. 27.*

When I loosen my grip on the pen, it slips from my hand and whips away in an arc. Gravity is strange here. It doesn't behave the way you expect.

Shutting the album, I consider whether to mark my mission complete or incomplete. The pounding of my heart is making a *whoosh, whoosh* sound in my ears, but I follow Coach's instructions. I breathe. I think.

If I mark the assignment incomplete, Miss Rose might ask Alia why she was unable to perform such a simple task. I'll have to tell Alia I couldn't do it—which is going to make *her* ask questions—and ultimately, Alia will have to lie to Miss Rose.

Too complicated.

I push Complete and the assignment vanishes from Alia's bracelet. I stare at the screen, horrified. I've taken another

Agent's assignment, marked it complete when it isn't, and stolen something from the site of a course correction.

I've broken almost every rule there is for an Agent. But if nothing in my life is what I thought it was—not my birth parents or my adoptive parents, not Miss Rose or the Seers—then what is the point of *rules*?

5. JADIE

Traveling through 4-space, I clutch the album tightly, but as soon as I land in my bedroom, I toss it onto the bed like it's a grenade. It lands with a soft *whomp* on the comforter and lies there, mocking me.

For several seconds, I stare at it with my arms drawn against my chest.

I'm wrong. I'm crazy. I'm going to be in so much trouble. I discovered something really bad.

Jadie 2.0 tells me to knock off the hysterics and get to work. Sinking onto the bed, I open the album cover again.

For my daughter, Jocelyn Dakota Lowell.

The newborn is swaddled in a hospital blanket on the first few pages, so I pass by those pictures. I pay more attention when the baby is uncovered and dressed in short sleeves, but none of the photos give me as good a view of the birthmark as that family portrait in the apartment. For the most part, I keep my eyes on Jocelyn, who grows bigger page by page. I'm curious about the parents and the boy but refuse to give them too much attention until—and *unless*—I prove they're important to me.

But the more I thumb through the album, the less connected to it I feel. There's no evidence this baby is me. I'm sure I've made a silly mistake based on a coincidence, and somehow, I'll have to put my theft right. Maybe confess to Miss Rose, and . . .

I freeze, staring at a caption beneath one of the pictures.

Sam can't pronounce your name. I want to call you Josie for short, but your daddy suggested J.D. and since Sam is learning his letters, he thinks that's a great name. I am outvoted.

J.D.

Jadie.

When my parents rescued me from that snowbank twelve years ago, I was approximately one year old and knew three words: *kitty*, *baba* for bottle, and *jadie*, which Mom and Dad decided was my name.

Every hair on my body stands on end. I flip directly to the back of the album, skipping everything else to find out what happened, and discover . . . nothing. No explanation. The photos stop two-thirds of the way through the book, with only blank pages following. The last picture shows the boy blowing out candles on a cake while the dad holds the girl up to see. In this picture, her birthmark is plain and clear, and I have no doubt it's mine.

Sam's 3rd birthday, the caption reads. *Next up is yours.*

Not *Tomorrow we're going to abandon you in a snowstorm.*

Maybe that isn't what happened. It can't be.

I jump up and circle the room, needing to burn off the energy churning in my body. This album holds the story of the earliest days of my life. But it doesn't hold *the* story—the one that explains how I got from these pictures to the arms of my adopted parents, Darrien and Becca Martin. The mother didn't write that story down.

The mother.

That's how I'm thinking about the people in this album. *The mother. The father. The brother.* I can't bring myself to give them more personal titles—titles that belong to three other people in my life. I glance at their faces but avoid really looking.

Worst of all, the inner core of *me* is screaming behind a glass wall, pounding with her fists against the barrier. For now, I imagine that wall as soundproof. This has to stay impersonal until I find out who the Lowells are and what happened to J.D.

Throwing myself in front of my laptop, I Google variations of that name. Jocelyn Dakota Lowell. J. D. Lowell. I finally get a hit on Jocelyn Lowell—a link to an article with an Amber

Alert title. The twelve-year-old link is broken, but Jocelyn Lowell must have been kidnapped or they wouldn't have put out an alert on her.

An electronic chirp interrupts my thoughts: text notification on my phone. When I check, the message is from Alia.

Ack! Parents coming home early OMW

Alia is on her way to retrieve her bracelet. My eyes automatically shoot to the baby album and its incriminating photos. I don't want Alia coming to my room and seeing that, so I unsnap her bracelet and race to meet her downstairs.

In the hallway, I collide with Marius coming out of the bathroom. It's only a small bump, but he staggers backward, one hand on his stomach and the other going to his head. "Sorry," I say, hurrying past him. But then I stop and give him another look. His normally olive complexion has gone pale, his forehead is shiny with sweat, and there's something weird about his hair. "Are you sick?"

"No," he mumbles before turning away from me and walking straight into a decorative table. "Oops."

"What did Ty make you do?" My brother was fine earlier,

but now he's absolutely green. Did he smoke a cigar? Drink something from Dr. Rivers's liquor cabinet?

At the mention of Ty, Marius glances at a scrap of paper in his hand before trying to shove it into his pocket. He misses but doesn't notice it fluttering to the floor because he's too busy staring at his closed bedroom door like it's a complex Chinese puzzle box. He reaches out to rotate the doorknob. With his left hand. The wrong way. *Twice.*

I groan as the realization hits me. "You dummy." Now I see what's wrong with his hair. It's parted on the wrong side. "You reversed yourself."

"Uhhh . . ." Thinking up a lie is too much for Marius. He stares at me pitifully.

Hauling my helpless, *backward* brother away from the door, I open it for him and guide him in. "Why'd you do this? You *know* how you react to it."

"Ty said he thought I could get used to it." While Marius stumbles toward his bed, I scoop up the paper he dropped and tuck it into my own pocket. Marius looks around the room, which appears reversed to his brain, then moans and falls over on his side.

Reversing is similar to the flips they teach us in geometry class—where you imagine a two-dimensional shape lifting off the paper and turning over. It becomes a mirror image of itself.

The same thing can happen to a human when we're lifted out of our universe. That's why we're supposed to *always* wear our bracelets on the left arm. If we switched, the Transporter might accidentally flip us and return us to Earth with our heart and other organs on the wrong side of our bodies.

Marius and I knew about the possibility of reversal from our parents long before we were Agents. But Miss Rose made a point of discussing it when she trained me, Marius, Ty, and Alia late last year.

Our 4-space liaison brought us together in Alia's family rec room to begin our lessons. That is, the four of us kids were in the room. As a 4-space being, Miss Rose doesn't fit in a human dwelling any more than a human could fit inside a two-dimensional universe as thin as a sheet of paper. (Miss Rose says such universes exist but their life-forms haven't evolved beyond amoebas.) During the lessons, her disembodied voice filtered into Alia's rec room from someplace outside three-dimensional space.

"There is no chance of *accidental* reversal as long as you follow procedure," she explained. "Those of you tempted to experiment by switching your bracelets to the other arm might wonder what it feels like. For some, nothing would be different. Most humans, however, experience severe nausea and lack of coordination. The condition is remedied by returning to 4-space and flipping back. Even for people unaffected by the change, reversing yourself is not recommended. It would be detrimental to the Seers' plans if a reversed individual was examined by a doctor. The secrecy of our activities is vital. Do you understand?"

"Yes, Miss Rose," we chorused, knowing that each of us was going to reverse ourselves as soon as we possibly could.

I did it during my second solo assignment and landed back on Earth with my birthmark on my right arm instead of the left. When I looked around, the world seemed perfectly normal.

Marius tried it later the same day and managed only a few steps before throwing up on his shoes.

I wasn't around when Alia and Ty made their attempts, but I know that Ty was walloped with a migraine and Alia sat down on the ground and refused to move until Miss Rose rescued her. It was impossible to switch back without help from the fourth dimension. They either summoned Miss Rose and confessed, or their parents did it for them. I was the only one who got away with it. I wore long sleeves until my next course correction, then unreversed myself. The adults thought I was the only kid virtuous enough to follow directions.

Now I'm going to have to call Miss Rose to come flip Marius back to normal. I lift the bracelet in my hand to look for the little recessed button that summons her and remember at the last second that it isn't mine.

Downstairs, the doorbell rings. Alia.

My stomach lurches as it hits me again. My birthmark. The photo album in my room. What I know that I can't unknow. I don't want to call Miss Rose. She's the last person in or out of my universe that I want to see right now. "Marius, you're going to have to call Miss Rose yourself."

"No!" Marius lifts his head off the bed. "She'll lecture me on *blah, blah* security and *blah, blah* the future of the human race. Leave me alone. I'll take care of it."

"*How?* You think you can stay like this until your next course correction?" Agents can't call on the Transporter whenever we want. The connection is only activated when a course correction is transmitted to our bracelets, and it lasts until we request transport home. If Marius has already completed a course correction today—which he must have, since he reversed himself—he won't get another until tomorrow at the soonest.

"Don't worry about me," Marius groans. "I've got this."

Downstairs, Mom calls, "Ja-die! Alia's here for you!"

I flinch, hearing my name dragged out so that it sounds like those initials. *J.D.* "Suit yourself," I tell Marius, heading for the door.

"Don't tell Mom!"

"I won't."

As much as I don't want to face Miss Rose right now, Mom and Dad are a close second. *How much of the truth about Jocelyn Lowell do they know?*

6. JADIE

In the foyer at the bottom of the staircase, I find Mom chatting amiably with Alia. Mom doesn't look like a diabolical kidnapper. Her sunglasses are perched on top of her head where she put them when we left the soccer field. I'm one hundred percent certain she's forgotten they're there and will be searching for them within the next half hour.

She also doesn't seem to notice how Alia keeps glancing over her shoulder and shifting from foot to foot. Alia wants to finish her business with me and beat her parents home, but Mom blathers on. "If your mother can make her famous egg yolk tarts for the bake sale, that would be perfect. If not, maybe the sweet bread she brought to the New Year's party?"

"Uh-huh." Alia's eyes dart toward me. "Oh, here she is! Excuse us, Mrs. Martin." She grabs me by the arm and drags me out the front door. "Do you have it?" she whispers as soon as we're outside. I extend the bracelet, which she snatches from my hand. "Do you think your mom will tell mine that I was here while I was grounded?"

"She has no idea you're grounded. But you better pass along that message about the bake sale and say my mom called your house. Because if your mom doesn't turn up with those tarts and they start talking . . ."

"Yeah, good thinking."

It *is,* which is a little alarming because I don't usually scheme and lie. Why am I suddenly good at it? I brace myself for Alia to ask whether I covered a course correction for her, but she darts down my front steps and sprints toward home without thanking me. My annoyance is tempered by the realization that if she hadn't asked me for this favor . . . I still wouldn't know where I came from.

Mom has retreated to the kitchen when I go back inside. I take the stairs two at a time and pass by Marius's closed door without a twinge of guilt. His problem is of his own making. Mine is not.

This time when I pick up the baby album, I read through it carefully. To make it easier to handle, I pretend it's not *me* in the pictures, just some kid named J.D.

The mother—Mrs. Lowell—assembled the album for her daughter to read in the future. She wrote in first person, referring to herself as *I* and her husband as *your daddy,* never mentioning their names or where they lived. The pages cover J.D.'s milestone moments: her first smile, her first word (*kitty*), and what day she started crawling. The kitty in question isn't the one I saw at the apartment, but a fat, elderly-looking tabby that probably isn't among the living anymore. There are pictures of the Lowells taking baby J.D. to a zoo, but I can't tell *which* zoo.

When I come across a picture of J.D. sitting on her father's lap at his desk, I get out a magnifying glass. The titles of the books on the shelf above his workspace are science and math related. Mr. Lowell could be a teacher, a scientist, or an engineer.

Next I turn my attention to J.D.'s brother. If he had his third birthday when J.D. was almost a year old, he'd be fifteen now, so I search Instagram, Snapchat, and Facebook. I eliminate most of the Sam Lowells I find—some of the Sams are the wrong age or the wrong race, and some are Samanthas. A few, I can't tell. My gut feeling is that none match the boy in this album.

I turn back to the photos, and that glass window between Jadie 2.0 and Hysterical Me cracks a bit. *Look at them! Really look at them! These are your birth parents! That boy is your brother!*

Mrs. Lowell has chin-length blond hair, and in every picture, she's smiling at the camera. There's one shot of her with Sam and J.D. dressed in Christmas sweaters where Mrs. Lowell holds J.D. on her hip and J.D. is throwing a full-blown tantrum. The baby's mouth is open wide, her eyes squeezed shut, her fists clenched angrily in the air. But Mrs. Lowell smiles brightly.

Underneath the photo, she wrote: *You were offended by our ugly Christmas sweaters.*

Mr. Lowell looks less comfortable in front of the camera than his wife. His smile is self-conscious, and the camera often catches him in the middle of pushing up his glasses. My favorite picture of him is from when J.D. is very small. Mr. Lowell is sprawled on a sofa. His glasses are perched on top of his head, and his light brown hair looks like a bird's nest. Sam is on his lap, eyes closed, dozing. And J.D. is on *Sam's* lap, taking a bottle from her father.

The caption: *You woke <u>everybody</u> up early this morning!*

Tears sting my eyes. I wipe them away, angry that this book is making me cry. I don't remember these people. Nothing in these photos is familiar. But I can tell I was loved.

These people didn't abandon me. I was kidnapped.

Then what? Did the kidnapper leave me in the snow? The Seers arranged my rescue from certain death and instructed Darrien and Becca Martin to take me home and raise me as their own. Why didn't the Seers have them take me to the police or to a hospital where I could be reunited with my family?

Once I start questioning the Seers, it's a slippery slope. Like, if it was possible to rescue Marius from a burning house, why not the rest of his family?

We've always assumed his parents are dead. What if they're not?

Hysterical Me has stopped banging on the glass wall in my brain, and turns out, she wasn't hysterical at all. *See what I was trying to tell you? This is bad. You discovered something reeeeeally baaaaaad.*

Questioning the Seers is discouraged. Miss Rose says human brains aren't wired to untangle the complexity of course corrections, just as our eyes aren't built to see ana or kata.

"Time is visible in both directions to the Seers," Miss Rose explained. "They see backward and forward and sometimes both at the same time. Your species cannot perceive causality the way ours does."

Either the Seers know where I came from and chose to separate me from my family—or they don't know as much as they claim they do. In which case, what's *really* happening when I steal some woman's bag and throw it into the street? Or pour a glass of water on someone's computer?

A chill runs up my back as I remember why I was in that apartment to start with. The Seers sent Alia to destroy Sam Lowell's computer. Why?

At that moment, Dad calls for dinner with his usual method: bellowing up the stairs. "Jadie, Marius, dinner!"

I shut the book and shove it under my bed, out of sight. For good measure, I close my laptop, hiding my incriminating Google searches.

The scent of pizza greets me before I reach the kitchen, as do my parents' voices. Entering the room, I glance their way, worried they'll appear different to my eyes. Mom as a human trafficking genius. Dad as kidnapper extraordinaire.

But they look like themselves. Some people think they make an odd couple because my mom is a tall redhead with the build of a female wrestler (she's actually a bookkeeper), and my dad is a short and pudgy Black guy who thinks an earring makes him edgier than your average history professor. (It doesn't.) I've heard people call them Mutt and Jeff, and I had to look that up, but the point is, they're ordinary. You'd never guess they're also agents for superintelligent four-dimensional beings. At the moment, Mom is fussing at Dad for bringing home pizzas after she went to the store. "I was making a chef's salad. I bought grilled chicken strips and—"

"Chef's salad? The kids won their games this morning. They don't want salad."

"You mean *you* don't want it."

Dad winks at me. "Congratulations on your game, Jadie-bean."

"Thanks." I avoid his gaze, looking at the pizza instead.

I've had nothing to eat since that lousy burrito, but I'm not hungry. "Marius won his game too?"

"Of course we did." Marius drops into the chair across from me. "I was pitching, wasn't I?"

My mouth flops open. Marius's complexion is back to normal, and his hair is parted on the correct side. His dark eyes shoot a laser-beam message at me.

Don't say anything.

7. JADIE

Marius stares at me intensely, and I drop my eyes first.

How did he unreverse himself without calling Miss Rose?

Assuming he reversed himself during a course correction, the only way for him to get back to 4-space the same day would be to borrow a friend's bracelet and hope a mission appeared when he needed it.

How likely is that?

Remembering the scrap of paper Marius dropped on the floor, I ease it out of my pocket and unfold it under the table. I'm not surprised to see a long string of numbers that look like Transporter coordinates.

"You okay, Jadie?" Mom asks. "Aren't you hungry?"

I lift my head. Mom and Dad are both pointedly eyeing my empty plate. Marius has taken two slices, one from each pizza, and on any other day, I would've wrestled him for the pieces with the most toppings. I help myself to a slice of mushroom–black olive and a slice of pepperoni-sausage to match my brother, even though I don't want either. "Just distracted. A school assignment has me stumped." I glare across the table at Marius. "But I'll figure it out."

Marius gazes with pretended fascination at the light fixture overhead, chewing noisily.

I'm onto you, brother.

About a month ago, on a Saturday afternoon, I heard a commotion through my bedroom window and pulled up the blinds. Next door, Dr. Rivers was yelling at Ty. Apparently, Ty had dropped his bracelet in the backyard and crushed it so thoroughly with the lawn mower that it was unrecognizable.

"I ask you to do *one* thing," Dr. Rivers shouted. "*One* thing to pull your weight around here, and you manage to destroy your bracelet? Of all the stupid, careless things ... This is an embarrassment for the Seers!"

Ty leaned away from his father like the Tower of Pisa, saying nothing and staring across the yard as if pretending to be somewhere else. I remember thinking that Dr. Rivers didn't know his son very well because Ty isn't stupid *or* careless. He probably crushed the bracelet on purpose because he'd been tinkering with it and didn't want anyone to know.

I hadn't thought about it much at the time, but it seems significant now.

Ty pulverized his bracelet and had to be given a new one. Today, he had a project he wanted Marius to help him with, during which it seems like Marius reversed and unreversed himself while carrying Transporter coordinates in his pocket.

The Transporter moves Agents from place to place on Earth, getting us to our destination in seconds because the machine itself is located outside our three-dimensional space. I knew what it did long before I started training as an Agent, since my parents used it every day. But it was Miss Rose who explained how it works.

By that point in our training, Miss Rose had started using an avatar—a three-dimensional puppet that stood in for her. We all blamed Marius, who'd complained that being taught by a disembodied voice was *freaky*. The avatar was not an improvement, being a mannequin that stared at us with unblinking eyes and a creepy, fixed smile.

"On the table," the avatar said without moving its mouth, "you will find a maze and a pencil. Please put your pencil tips on the starting point and, when I say *go*, move through the maze without lifting the pencil until you reach the exit."

Marius and I exchanged glances, preparing to race each other. But it was Ty who completed the puzzle first.

"Moving from one end of the maze to the other takes time, and your pencil travels some distance," Miss Rose said when we finished. "But that time and distance only apply if you follow two-dimensional rules. Put your pencils at the starting point again." Everyone did. "Lift your pencils up, move them directly to the end point, and put them down again." We did as we were told. "That took less time, and the pencil traveled a smaller distance because you lifted the pencil out of two-dimensional space. That is what the Transporter does. It takes you on a shortcut—kata out of your world, and ana back."

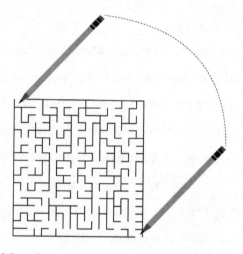

Alia raised her hand. "Can it work the other way? Ana out of this world and kata back?"

"Good question." Miss Rose's avatar turned its whole body toward Alia and bobbed, the closest it could come to nodding. "Put your pencil on the starting point of the maze again. Move it down and *then* up."

I stared at my paper, uncertain how to follow those instructions.

"She means like this." Ty lifted the paper slightly off the table and stabbed his pencil straight through it.

"Exactly right, Ty," said Miss Rose. "Reversing the ana and kata directions during Transportation is possible, but not advisable. Your universe is delicate. You must trust that we know the best way to nurture it."

You must trust. We hear that a lot from Miss Rose. Up until now, I did trust.

If Mom and Dad aren't as innocent as they seem at dinner tonight, that means they collaborated with Miss Rose to take me from the Lowells. If I show them J.D.'s album, the first thing they'll do is consult her on what to do, now that I've discovered the truth. My parents have been Agents for Miss Rose since she first recruited them in college two decades ago. In fact—innocent *or* guilty—confronted with that album, they'll turn immediately to Miss Rose for advice. And I don't think that would be a good idea.

My eyes travel toward my brother. He's watching me while pretending not to and probably wondering if I've figured out his secret. I have, but I'm reluctant to involve him in *my* secret until I know more about who the Lowells are, why the Seers separated me from them, and how this impacts my family.

So I won't ask Marius for help (yet), but I might get something useful from a person I dislike. He dislikes me too, though he'll trade information without asking too many questions as long as he thinks he's getting the better end of the deal.

8. JADIE

"To what do I owe the honor of this visit?" Ty asks, his eyes on his computer.

I glare at his back.

He didn't turn around to face me when Mrs. Rivers showed me to his room, which is as creepy as I expected. It's weirdly neat compared to Marius's room or Sam Lowell's. Everything is clean and in its place, but there are horror movie posters on the walls, a pet snake in a glass cage, a partially dismantled robot dog, and a baby shark preserved in a glass jar. Gross.

"Ahem," I say.

Ty swivels around in his chair and tosses his long bangs out of his face. "Ahem? Did you actually *say* 'ahem'?"

Do people not say that? It's written in books when a person wants to attract someone's attention. My cheeks burn.

"Did you want something?" he asks. "Or did you come by just to drop a little onomatopoeia into my day?"

This is why Ty is my next-door nemesis. I force myself to relax my jaw. Unfolding a Post-it note, I show him the string of numbers I copied from Alia's bracelet. "These are the coordinates for a course correction. Do you have any way of identifying the location?"

At first, he leans back in his chair and says nothing. Ty has a way of making it look like he's falling asleep while you're talking to him, which irritates both his peers and his teachers. I wait him out, and eventually he admits, "I might. Let me see."

I hand the Post-it over. He sticks the paper to his desk and opens a file on his computer. "I've been fooling around with these numbers for a while now." Over his shoulder, I see a spreadsheet with coordinates entered into columns, along with place names and other descriptions, like *on the street* or *in a second-floor stairwell.*

"Has Marius been helping you collect these?"

He enters my numbers into the spreadsheet without answering. "Do you know where you were?"

"An apartment in the US, I think. Can't you tell me where I was, from the numbers?"

"Correlating known locations with the numbers is what's helping me figure it out."

"Can you give me an area of the country?"

Ty swings around in his chair again, making me jump back. "Why does Miss Perfect Jadie Martin want to read the Seers' code?"

"I'm not perfect."

"Straight-A student. Soccer star. Popular in school. Of course, I'm sure it's overcompensation for being abandoned as a baby."

I raise my fist. "How about I pop you in the mouth? That wouldn't be perfect."

"Everybody would assume you had a good reason." He turns back to his computer, closes the spreadsheet, and opens a window filled with weird programming language.

"Well?" I ask.

"Before I give you any information," he says, "I want you to tell me something."

"What?"

"*Why* do you want to know this?"

"Why do you need to know why I want to know?"

"It's my price." Ty types in a few lines of code and scans the screen. "If you're coming to me with this instead of asking Marius, there must be a reason."

I knew there'd be a price, but I thought he'd ask for a future alibi or my firstborn child, like Rumpelstiltskin. Clenching my teeth, I fantasize about hitting him over the head with that shark-in-a-jar. "I saw something that interests me. I want to know where it was."

"You want to go back to that spot?"

"No. Like I said, it's in the middle of somebody's apartment. I want to know where in the country it is. Is it a bus ride from here? Or a plane ride?"

"Must have been something pretty interesting."

I turn around and head for the door. "Forget it. I don't need you." A pulse in my throat reminds me that I *do* need him. Walking out is a bluff.

"Ho-o-o-old on." Ty drags out the words like he doesn't really care if I leave—but I think he's bluffing too. "Do you have your bracelet?"

"Yeah."

"Good." Taking something from his desk that looks like a wand attached to a small box, he stands up and gestures with his hand. Reluctantly, I raise my arm. Ty grabs it, turns the bracelet around on my wrist, and touches the wand to a specific spot.

"What'd you do?"

"Called for a ride." He pushes the button on my bracelet with his thumb.

Before I can react, I'm yanked kata, out of the room. The world contracts to a squished line and vanishes. My bracelet clicks into a port-lock on the Transporter. A few seconds later,

Ty lands beside me, his bracelet connecting with the port-lock on an adjacent platform. I reach across the gap and punch him in the arm with my free hand.

He yelps. "Ooouuw! Isthathoooo yutreeee tagiiii dingya faaaaavooooor?"

It takes a few seconds for me to understand what he said. In 4-space, sound waves travel differently than they do on Earth. You get the hang of untangling words after your brain adjusts.

What Ty said was: *Ow! Is that how you treat a guy doing you a favor?*

"You hijacked the Transporter!" After Marius's stunt this afternoon, I'd suspected he could do this, but it's still a shock. "We're going to—"

I bite off the rest of my sentence, but he guesses what I was going to say and sneers at me. "We're *not* going to get in trouble, Miss Perfect." He throws back his head and hollers, "Hey, Seers! Come and get me!"

I glance around warily, but 4-space is full of the same unidentifiable globs it always is.

"Nobody's watching," Ty says. "I come here all the time."

"How?"

"There's an optical coupler in the bracelets that gets activated when we receive a course correction, which is delivered through old pager technology from some guy working in a customer support center. I traced the signal back to his computer, hacked it, and found the code."

It takes more than a couple of seconds to untangle *those* words, but I've seen pagers on old TV shows. What he's saying is that someone pages our bracelets with a course correction, and the signal activates contact with the Transporter. In spite of myself, I'm impressed. "I knew you didn't pulverize your old bracelet by accident. You took it apart to find out how it worked."

"The Seers aren't as advanced as we think," Ty says. "The Transporter isn't very sophisticated either. Isn't that a gear? And that looks like a roller chain."

He points at a clunky thing to our left that's metallic and jagged, and something else above it. They *might* be a gear and a chain, but it's impossible to be sure. Our eyes can't see the entirety of four-dimensional objects, only cross-sections of them. It's like handing a sliver of pineapple to someone who's never seen one before and expecting them to know what the whole fruit looks like.

"You know what?" Ty grins at me. "I think the bracelets are on a four-dimensional fishing line. The Transporter reels us in and casts us out."

"It can't be that simple."

"It might be."

Normally, I'd tell Ty that I don't care how the Transporter works, just that it does. But that's not true anymore. Everything he's saying supports what I've started to suspect. Miss Rose and the Seers have been feeding Agents platter after platter of baloney sandwiches.

"It's completely automated," Ty continues. "All the times I've come up here unauthorized, Miss Rose has never said a word to me."

"Marius comes too, doesn't he? This is how he got reversed." The four-dimensional sound waves don't conceal my disapproval.

"He wanted to see if he could get used to it. Stop acting like Marius is a helpless dolt. You are so *superior* sometimes, Jadie."

I'm positive Marius said it was Ty who encouraged him to reverse himself, but I don't bother arguing. "Why'd you bring me out here?"

"I can take you to those coordinates." Ty fishes the Post-it out of his pocket. "You don't need a plane or a bus ride to get there."

"I *told* you. It's someone's apartment. If we show up at the wrong time, we'll be seen. I'd like to get close to the spot, but not exactly there. Can you do that?"

Ty shakes his head. "I think these numbers are similar to

longitude and latitude, but we only need two coordinates to identify locations on Earth. The Seers use four, which makes sense because they can place us down in a subway, on a street, or up on the twentieth floor of a building. If I change one of these numbers even slightly, I might bury us in a wall or drop us from fifty feet in the air. Your numbers won't help me figure out their system if you have no idea where you were."

I heave a sigh. "What do you want from me?"

A hungry gleam sparks in his eyes. "Your mission coordinates. All of 'em. With as much information about their physical locations as you can figure out. That apartment you were in—if you'd looked out the window to see what floor you were on, it would've told me *something*. Every piece of information I get helps me break their code."

I wonder what he plans to do with the code if he breaks it, but I doubt he'd tell me the truth if I asked. "If I do that, you'll find this place for me?"

"That's the idea."

"It's a deal."

9. SAM

When Sam's father drags his suitcase into the apartment, bad news is visible in the slump of his shoulders. "Hey, son, how are things?"

Things are not good, but Sam doesn't want to hit his dad with the situation the moment he walks in the door. "Did it go well?" he asks instead. The answer is obvious, but *not asking* makes it seem like failure was expected.

His father shakes his head. "They were nice about it. Gave me some leads on other jobs. Hang on a second. I'm dying of thirst." He disappears into the kitchenette. "How's your knee?"

"Fine," Sam lies. He shifts his laptop to the coffee table and waits, jittering his good leg up and down.

Ice clatters into a glass. Water runs from the tap. "It isn't the end of the world," his dad says. "We'll tighten our belts. The internet has to go. You can use the Wi-Fi at the library, right?"

Inconvenient, but doable. "Sure, Dad. But there's something else..."

His father returns with a glass of water and sees what's wrong. "What the...? Were you and your mother rearranging the furniture?"

Sam sighs. The bookshelves have been pulled away from the wall. The closet is open, with its contents dumped on the floor. "J.D.'s baby album is missing."

"Missing? What do you mean, missing?"

"Mom noticed it wasn't on top of the bookshelf. We thought it might've fallen behind, but it wasn't there. So she pulled the place apart looking for it."

"But how could…" Sam's father waves a hand as if to ask how the album could move itself into the closet, but his voice tapers off because he knows how. Just like Sam knows.

"She says someone stole it."

Dad shoos the cat off the sofa and sits down next to Sam. Removing his glasses, he cleans them with his shirttail. "Where is she?"

"Asleep. Finally." It had required all Sam's powers of persuasion to convince her to take her pills. "Dad, I looked everywhere. I don't know what Mom did with the album."

Dad winces and closes his eyes.

What other explanation is there? A burglar stole pictures of a child who's been missing for years and is presumed dead? Mom won't remember hiding the book; her actions are a symptom of her paranoid delusion. But that doesn't make it easier to deal with.

Sam barely remembers his baby sister, but he does remember the tumult when J.D. disappeared. His mother had temporarily vanished from his life too. Though the injuries she received that day hadn't been life-threatening, her emotional state landed her in the hospital.

In the twelve years since, Sam has watched his mother relapse every time something bad happens to their family. Like when a hit-and-run driver clipped Sam's bike and he tore his ACL. Or when a random stranger on a plane got the job his mom wanted. She believes sinister, nameless enemies are out to destroy her family, and nothing has ever been able to convince her otherwise.

"I'll call her doctor." Dad puts his glasses on and pushes them up his nose. "Don't worry."

Don't worry? Sam's stomach burns with acid. Dad's unemployment checks barely cover food and rent, let alone doctors. He's paying for Mom's meds by credit card, and cutting off the internet isn't going to make a dent in that growing bill. The longer Sam's parents go without jobs, the deeper his family sinks into a bottomless hole of debt and the further his mother spirals into paranoia.

Sam would happily work if he could, but jobs are hard to find when you're a fifteen-year-old boy with an injured leg. His eyes wander back to the laptop.

"How's the project going?" his father asks, interpreting his son's gaze.

"About as good as everything else." Sam reaches for the computer and lifts it onto his lap. "I thought making a three-D model of the impossible cube would help. But it didn't solve my problem. I can't use the same strategy to create my Escher buildings on the screen."

Sam has been an M. C. Escher fanatic since he was seven, when his dad gave him a set of the artist's best drawings, including the *Belvedere* that still hangs in his room. "A structure like this is impossible in our universe," Dad said to young Sam when he pinned up the print. "But my job is studying dimensional universes where this building makes sense."

For a long time, Sam thought that meant his dad worked in the *Belvedere* building.

In reality, Sam's dad is a theoretical physicist compiling his own universal theory. When Sam was old enough to understand, his father was happy to explain. "Scientists have equations that describe how large objects like suns and planets move, but the equations don't work on tiny things like atoms. Other scientists have equations that explain what atoms do, but they don't apply to suns and planets. What I believe is that both sets of equations are part of a much bigger set of mathematics. We're like the three blind men in the story who lay hands on an elephant without knowing what one looks like. One touches the tail, another the trunk, and the third feels only the side of the elephant. My job is describing the whole elephant when I only have access to those little pieces."

Sam's own interest in Escher's work has always been for its visual appeal rather than dimensional physics. And when the coding program fell into his hands, he immediately thought of *Belvedere*.

Six months ago, after the bicycle accident ruined any chance of him joining the track team, his computer teacher offered him use of the program. "A college buddy runs a video game start-up company, and this software is on the cutting edge of graphics coding technology," the teacher explained. "I don't have time to work with it, but you've got the programming skills and the drive, and it'll keep you busy while you recuperate."

So, mostly out of boredom, Sam used the program to create the beginnings of a world with impossible geometry: Möbius strip roads, buildings built from impossible cubes, creatures that tessellate from flat to multidimensional and back again. When he shared his preliminary design with his teacher, it became apparent that the gift had been more than a way for Sam to pass the time.

"My buddy *loves* what you did!" the teacher exclaimed to Sam in a follow-up phone call. "Says there's nothing out there like it! If you complete this multidimensional landscape, you'll be paid for the design." He named a price that made Sam's heart leap.

"It's a landscape, not a whole game," Sam felt obligated to remind his teacher. "And does he know I'm only fifteen?"

"He likes working with young talent, and he doesn't underpay them, the way some businessmen might. He's got a college-age kid who'll work with you on the plot of the game and another who'll write the dialogue. If this comes to fruition, you'll get your name in the credits and a percentage of the royalties. First you have to make that landscape work."

Now it was more than a pastime. It was income his family sorely needed. But as Sam tried to flesh out his original idea, he immediately hit a wall.

Showing his father the gaps and glitches where his landscape is full of *holes*, he explains, "No matter how I enter the data, the program can't figure out how to display the buildings from different angles. Maybe it can't be done."

His father moves the computer onto his own lap. "Let me look at the code. There isn't anything that can't be done if you think about it the right way."

Except convince Mom there's no secret organization out to get us. Sam suppresses his sigh.

After scanning several pages of code, Dad frowns. "This software is designed to make two-dimensional images fool the brain into thinking they're three-dimensional. But you're trying to make them look four-*dimensional*, and this program has no idea what that means."

Sam thunks his head against the back of the sofa. "So it's hopeless."

"I didn't say that. This software may have the capacity to learn. I've been working on a mathematical application of ana and kata. If you trust me with your laptop, I'll upload my math tonight."

"Of course I trust you," says Sam. "But, um..." His eyes wander toward the bedrooms.

His father's face falls. "If I have time. We'll see how she is."

Taking care of Mom comes first. But they need money to get her proper care, and selling this game design is the only way Sam can help. It's a shame Mom did something to his sister's photo album, but, in Sam's opinion, there are worse things she could have done.

Second only to his father's brilliant mind, the content on this laptop might be the most valuable thing in their apartment.

10. JADIE

Three days go by without a course correction. Actually, four—because the one on Saturday was Alia's, not mine.

I was so shaken on Saturday that I didn't notice I got no assignment of my own. On Sunday, I kept checking my bracelet, especially during Coach's party, because that would've been the most inconvenient time. Nothing.

Monday . . . nothing. Today . . . nothing.

I've never gone four days without an assignment, and I can't shake the idea that the Seers *know*. I'm not sure *what* they know—that I took Alia's course correction and failed to do it, or that I found my birth family.

But if Miss Rose and the Seers know what I did, why haven't I been reprimanded? Waiting for a punishment is more agonizing than most punishments, which I guess is the reason for the famous water drip torture. By the end of three days, I'm a taut string, ready to snap.

After dinner, while Mom's running errands, Dad plunks a container of ice cream in front of me and hands me a spoon. "What's up, Jadie-bean?" He peels the lid off the container and digs his own spoon into it.

Mom hates people eating straight from the carton. Which is why, when Dad does it, it's supposed to be a *between you and me* thing. The kind that encourages me to confide in him.

I see right through his ploy, but I plunge my spoon into the Rocky Road anyway. I *wish* I could share my problem with him. Before I saw that family photograph in the Lowell apartment, the only secret I'd ever kept from my parents was their Christmas presents. For about the hundredth time, I consider showing him J.D.'s album . . .

The truth is, I'm scared.

Scared that Mom and Dad knew. That they were complicit in the kidnapping. Or—worse—that Mom and Dad are the good guys I've always known they are, and when they see the truth, they'll decide to find the Lowells and *give me back.* I might be horrified by J.D.'s kidnapping *in theory,* but this is my family now, and I don't want to trade them for some people in a photo album.

Since I can't directly tell Dad what the problem is, I approach it from another angle. "Do you ever wonder what your course corrections *do?*"

"Every day. But Miss Rose says it works better if we don't know. I've told you about my first assignment, when we were all in college?"

Dad and his friends Joe Rivers, Ada Malik, and Chen Li were students when Miss Rose first spoke to them from 4-space and made them aware of the higher-dimensional universe that surrounded their own. She convinced them to assist her in missions for the Seers by engaging them in what seemed, at first, like a pointless activity. I've heard the story before, but that doesn't stop Dad. He's a history professor. He *likes* telling stories over and over.

"Miss Rose plopped us in a dark office in the middle of the night and told us to—"

"Rearrange the furniture. I know."

"A week later, the US news was completely consumed by the assassination plot and how it was foiled. We wondered if it had something to do with us . . . but that seemed impossible. Until Miss Rose returned and explained it."

Dad and his friends moved furniture in the office of some woman who worked for an advertising firm. She must've been really confused when she came to work the next day. Her chair was now next to an air vent, and by a weird architectural flaw, she could hear the conversations of a man on the floor below her. When she overheard him talking about a huge cocaine deal, she confided in her boss, who notified the police.

The police raided the drug dealer's apartment and—completely by accident—startled a group of domestic terrorists in the apartment next door. Thinking *they* were being raided, they engaged in a gunfight with police and lost, and as a result, their scheme to assassinate the president was uncovered.

"The Valentine's Day Plot was the greatest event that never happened since Guy Fawkes failed to blow up the English Parliament in 1605," Dad says. "No one knew the coincidences that caused the assassination plan to be uncovered—except us. After that we were convinced." He shrugs. "Turns out, save the life of the president *one time,* and you end up hooked. Miss Rose never reveals the intended results of our course corrections, but sometimes we can guess. Joe told me recently that he was watching the news and recognized a man he saved from choking in a restaurant ten years ago. That man is now running for senator in Minnesota, so draw your own conclusions."

Sure. Ty's dad performs the Heimlich maneuver, and a decade later the guy becomes a senator. Hey, maybe he'll end up president. Good for him. That doesn't explain what happened to me and the Lowells.

Dad asks, "Did you do a course correction that bothers you?"

"I snatched a lady's bag and threw it into traffic."

He cringes. "Ones like that are tough. About six months

ago, I was instructed to walk into the street in front of an oncoming car."

I gulp. Stepping in front of a car would take a lot of guts—and a lot of trust in the Seers.

"The driver saw me and swerved. But he clipped a bike and knocked the boy riding it into the street. Then he drove off without stopping." Dad gazes over my shoulder like he's envisioning the scene. "I was horrified. I rushed over to help the boy, but he didn't seem to be hurt much. Shaken up, a few scrapes, that's all."

"Geez, Dad." What if the car hadn't swerved? What if the Seers had miscalculated and my dad got run over? This is not helping me with my trust issues, but Dad keeps eating his ice cream like he has no doubts whatsoever.

"It helps to remember we're working toward better lives for humankind. I don't know if what happened was meant to change the boy's life, or the driver's, or someone else entirely. But I trust it was for a good reason."

"Why? I mean, I know you saved the president once, but how are you still so sure?"

"Do you think überintelligent beings from a higher dimension would expend this much energy for anything less than a good reason? If they wanted to *hurt* us, they could do so. Easily. We'd never see it coming."

"People do things for dumb reasons." I think about Marius reversing himself and puking in the bathroom.

"True. But let me point this out: A cruel child might burn an anthill with a magnifying glass to watch the ants run. But he won't do it long before moving on to some other amusement. A caring child might buy an ant farm and watch them with fascination for years. I don't think the Seers would put this much effort into our world for anything other than our best interests."

I play with my spoon, twirling it this way and that. The Seers *see backward and forward and sometimes both at the same time.* That's what Miss Rose said.

But Ty told me, *Nobody's watching.*

Who's right?

Maybe both. The Seers might be capable of seeing all, but that doesn't mean they pay attention to every single thing. Not when there are billions of people to look at across time.

I glance warily at Dad before raising a more troubling subject. "Do you ever wonder what happened to the rest of Marius's family? Why did the Seers send you to save only him?"

Dad pauses a long time before answering. "Maybe it was impossible to save anyone else. Realistically, the Seers can't save the life of every person in danger."

I look down at my spoon again.

"I know this, Jadie-bean: *We're* Marius's family now. The Seers have given me two amazing children, and I'm proud of being father to both of you, even if you occasionally snatch purses from old ladies, or whatever."

The grin that overtakes me comes straight up from my heart. I'm proud to be his daughter too, and I can't imagine calling anyone else *Dad.*

Maybe the Seers do know best. Maybe I've got this wrong.

I've been researching Amber Alerts. They're not only issued in cases of kidnapping by a stranger, but also when the police suspect a child is in danger from an abusive or unstable relative. The Lowells *look* like a nice family, but who knows? Maybe those photos paint a false picture of my life with them.

Maybe, I think as Dad and I finish the ice cream and clean up the evidence, *I should stop worrying about* how *I got here and appreciate that I ended up here at all.*

Marius is bouncing a basketball in the driveway when I step outside to clear my head. "We never had that one-on-one," he calls out.

I put a hand over my ice cream–filled stomach. "Give me a minute."

"A minute to overcome your fear of *defeat*?" Marius catches the ball as it bounces off the asphalt. "A minute to say your *prayers*?"

Well, I'm not going to put up with that. I hold out my hands for the ball. "Say *your* prayers, Marius. Game on!"

Marius passes the ball, bouncing it once on the driveway between us. But my phone starts ringing in the back pocket of my jeans, and I let the ball sail past while I answer it. Ty's name appears on the screen. "Hello?"

"I've got a course correction with numbers close to that one of yours. Wanna go with me? In or out? Decide quick."

My head says *out*, but my mouth says, "In."

"Meet me at the playground behind our street."

I shove the phone back into my pocket and tell Marius, "Gotta go."

"Where?"

But I'm already running down the sidewalk—away from my home and my family, toward answers I shouldn't care about. Everything I decided in the kitchen with Dad flies right out the window.

I have to know more.

11. JADIE

"I almost didn't call you," Ty says when I show up at the playground, which was built for toddlers and is deserted in the evenings. "You haven't sent me any numbers."

"I haven't been on any course corrections," I answer breathlessly. "For days."

"That's weird."

"I thought maybe they found out about you taking me to 4-space."

"Not likely. I've had an assignment every day since then."

A fluttery sensation runs through me as I consider why I've been singled out. Covering my nervousness, I wave a hand at the plastic animals on giant springs and the three-foot-tall slide. "Why are we meeting here? Your house is a lot closer."

"Let's say I didn't want my mother seeing you come over again." Ty shows me his electric wand device. "This is how it's going to work: I'll activate your bracelet's communication to the Transporter, and when we get to 4-space, I'll enter our coordinates into the consoles. As soon as we arrive at our destination, the first thing we do is figure out where we are. Then I'll complete my assignment."

"How do I get home if we're separated for some reason?"

"Press the button for pickup, same as always. Once the Transporter has moved you, it's always available for a return trip."

"You're sure?"

"Done it lots of times. Geez. Who knew you were such a scaredy-cat?"

Five minutes and already my hands are bunched into fists. I force myself to tighten my ponytail with them instead of punching him. "Let's go."

Ty touches his device to my bracelet. I push the button myself, and moments later, I land on a platform in 4-space.

Wiping a sweaty hand on my pants, I wonder if I'm making a mistake. *I want to see where they are. Just so I know. One time, and then I'm done.* My left hand is immobilized in the port-lock, so I can't wipe it the way I want to, and I realize my birthmark is glaringly visible on that arm, identifying me as J.D. Lowell. If Ty's mission takes us near where the Lowells live, this could be a problem.

There's one thing I can do to disguise myself.

I unlatch my bracelet, turn a hundred and eighty degrees, and slip my right wrist into the metal ring instead. The Transporter will return me to Earth with the bracelet on my left, reversing my body, and the birthmark will end up on the opposite arm. It's not perfect, but it'll have to do.

The Transporter deposits Ty on the platform adjacent to mine, as it usually does when two Agents call for pickup at the same time and from the same place. His eyebrows shoot up under his long bangs when he sees me standing with my back to the console, my right arm in the bracelet. "Well, that's interesting."

I scowl at him. "Let's go. Okay?"

Chuckling, he stretches across the two-foot gap to punch my console keys. I crane my neck to watch him enter the numbers, but he does it too quickly for me to follow.

My platform moves away from his into the reddish gloom of 4-space. When it stops, the port-lock releases me, and I'm pulled ana back to Earth. The machine deposits me in a narrow space between two buildings. I look around, expecting Ty to appear, and then I remember he'll be entering the same coordinates. Hastily, I step backward.

Just in time. A thin line of substance appears in the spot where I was standing, then expands into Ty. "Glad you had the sense to get out of the way," he says. "Where are we?"

"In an alley."

"Ya think?"

We walk out to the street and find ourselves in a city. The streetlights are on, and it's a little darker than it was at home. *A different time zone. We're east of Kansas.* Most of the buildings on the street look residential, although there are a few businesses squeezed between them. Ty checks out the menu posted in the window of a sandwich shop. "We're in Philadelphia."

I point at a chalkboard propped on the sidewalk. PHILLY CHEESE STEAKS MADE 2 ORDER. "Ya think?" I use the same tone he used on me.

Ty glances at the sign, then takes out his phone. "Any restaurant can sell Philly cheese steaks or Chicago deep-dish pizza. Doesn't mean you're in Philadelphia or Chicago. The menu has an *address* on it."

He's right, darn him. While he snaps a picture of the address, I scan the residences on the street. Most of them are old buildings with their front doors located half a flight of stairs above street level. They're large enough to be subdivided into apartments. Although the evening is warm, I shiver, shifting from one foot to the other.

"Were you in one of those buildings?" Ty asks.

"I don't know. Maybe." But I'm thinking, *Yes!* My body feels something my mind doesn't understand. It's like, standing right here, right now, I'm caught between two worlds.

"I've never seen any two course correction numbers this close together before." Ty looks at the display on his bracelet and starts down the street, checking each car and parking meter as he goes. "I only started collecting them a few weeks ago, but this is the first time I know of two people going to the same place. If this is the same place." He looks back at me. "What'd you do? Mess up your job? Is that why you wanted to come back? To fix something?"

I don't answer. "What's your assignment?"

He stops in front of a blue Toyota Corolla, removes a quarter from his pocket, and inserts it into the parking meter. "The Seers want to save this guy from a ticket."

"Hey, you kids! Get away from there!" A woman in a police uniform stalks toward us. She glares at the timer, which now has ten minutes on it, then at Ty. "Get out of here! If I catch you doing that again, I'll write you up."

"For what?" Ty challenges her. "Doing a good deed?"

"Come on." I grab Ty by his shirt and pull him away. "Don't worry," I say to the woman. "He doesn't do good deeds often. They give him a rash."

"You know, they do make me itch a little." Ty scratches his armpit with one hand and his butt with the other.

"Do you have to be so gross?"

We retreat as far as the sandwich shop. "Now what?" Ty

asks. "You want to hang around and figure out which building you were in last time?"

I do and I don't. I stick my hands in my pockets, trying not to look at Ty, who stares at me like he thinks I've lost my mind. Maybe I have.

At that moment, the front door of the building beside the sandwich shop opens and a teenage boy walks out carrying a laptop under his arm. The boy from the photographs in the Lowell apartment.

My reversed heart pounds in the wrong side of my chest. Part of me wants to duck into the sandwich shop and hide; another part wants to stand here and stare at him. *All* of me wishes Ty weren't watching.

Sam is athletic-looking, but he moves slowly and gingerly, more like an older man than a fifteen-year-old boy. At the top of the steps, he switches the laptop to his other arm and grasps the railing before starting down. It looks like he's trying not to bend his left leg, and I remember the crutch in his room.

Behind him the front door of the building opens, and a man runs out, shouting, "Hey! Wait!"

Sam glances back, but the man isn't yelling at him. On the street, the grumpy meter maid has left the Corolla behind and is writing up a ticket for a RAV4 instead.

"It's almost eight o'clock! We don't have to feed the meters after eight!" The man pushes past Sam and runs to the street.

Sam's leg buckles, pitching him face-first down the stairs. One hand hangs on to the railing, but that doesn't stop his fall, and he has to use his other hand to catch himself. The laptop falls and slips through the railing.

My body dives forward like I'm blocking a soccer goal, and the computer lands squarely in my arms. Sam Lowell stares at me through the bars of the railing. "Caught it," I declare. "You okay?"

"I think so." He twists his body, trying to get to a sitting position.

"That guy didn't stop to see if you were hurt." I throw a dirty look at the man, who's arguing with the meter maid and either didn't notice what happened or doesn't care.

"Yeah. He lives in the apartment below me, and he's a jerk." Sam gets his head above his feet and settles himself on one of the steps. "Is my computer okay?"

"Should be." My hands tremble as I hand it up to him through the railing, and while I watch him examine it for damage, it hits me what I've done.

Alia's mission was to destroy that computer, but I didn't do it. So the Seers sent Ty, whose good deed resulted in another attack on the computer, which I prevented—again.

I've thwarted the Seers twice.

"Thanks for the catch." Sam looks at me again. His brow crumples, and his eyes—the same color and shape as mine—examine my face. "Do I know you?"

I clap a hand over the birthmark on my arm and back away. "Nope. Glad you're okay, but I gotta go."

Then I run.

Away from Sam.

Away from Ty, who stares at me with his mouth hanging open.

If I could, I'd run away from myself.

12. JADIE

The Transporter takes me back to the platform when I call for it, like Ty promised. I switch which arm is in the bracelet to unreverse myself and punch the button marked Return.

Ty is waiting in the playground with his arms crossed. "You undid my course correction," he says as soon as I appear.

"You don't know that," I snap. "You have no idea what putting a quarter in that meter was supposed to accomplish."

"Seems clear it was to get that kid knocked down the stairs and make his laptop smash on the ground. Nice catch, by the way."

My heart thumps. I don't like the glint of curiosity in his eyes, and I know I should act casual, like I don't care what happened and plan on never thinking about it again. Instead, I blurt out, "I'll fix it. Gimme that thing you use to call the Transporter, and I'll go back and fix what I did wrong."

"How are you going to do that?"

"I can . . ." Damn. Catching the laptop was a stupid thing to do. Interacting with Sam, even more stupid. I'm handling this *badly*.

"What was your last course correction?" Ty asks. "The one you messed up. Did it have to do with that boy? Do you know him?"

"How could I? He lives in Philadelphia. And I never said I messed up my course correction." Ty squints at me like he wants to know what makes me tick—which makes me think of the dismantled robot dog in his room and the bracelet he ran over with the lawn mower. I shiver and hold out my hand. "Give me that signaling device and the coordinates—"

"No. Not unless you tell me everything."

Why does he want to know? To have something to hold over me? Shoving my hands in my pockets, I walk away from him. It's not exactly another bluff, but I *am* hoping he'll call me back and offer a different deal.

He doesn't.

✳

Kidnappers. Amber Alerts. Important laptops.

Lies and more lies.

My life has turned into a conspiracy theory. And that's saying something, considering I was already a thirteen-year-old operative for beings from a higher dimension. But I've known about the Seers, the Transporter, and course corrections since I was little. That's *normal* for me.

Defying the Seers isn't.

It seems like the Lowells have been targeted for more than their fair share of course corrections. J.D. Lowell was lost, kidnapped, or otherwise separated from her family. Seers intervened to save her but didn't return her. Now they seem determined to wreck Sam's computer. What else have they done?

Miss Rose claims the Seers have a plan to benefit the human race. How do the Lowells fit in? Are they bad people? Russian spies pretending to be a normal American family?

I obsess about it the next day. Teachers reprimand me for not paying attention in class. Even Alia notices, and she's not the most observant person in the world. "What's wrong with you?" she asks at lunch. Her eyes never leave her handheld video game, but when I don't answer right away, she presses harder. "Spill it, Jadie. You're freaking me out. Your parents don't have cancer or something, do they?"

She's not freaked out enough to put the game down. "My parents are fine, thanks for asking." And then, because I don't know what to do, I tell her my problem. "I need information from Ty, and he won't give it to me."

I wait for her to ask what kind of information, but like the day I covered her course correction, she's not that curious.

Her thumbs rapidly press keys. "You know the saying, *When they go low, you go high?*"

"Yeah."

"That won't work on Ty. You have to go lower."

I blink. "Lower than Ty?"

"Go subterranean. You wouldn't use the Staff of Harmony against Malnoz the Poisonous Gas Bag, would you?" When I stare blankly at her, she lifts her eyes to me long enough to say, "Trust me. You wouldn't."

Go low. Well, I can't imagine going lower than involving Ty's dad. I've never liked Dr. Rivers, even though he's one of Dad's college friends. So after soccer practice, I head straight for the Rivers house without changing my clothes. When you've decided to do something distasteful, you want to get it over with as quickly as possible. They say snitches get stitches, but if I'm confronting a Poisonous Gas Bag (and I am), I'll have to hit him over the head with the Staff of Telling Your Dad.

Mrs. Rivers answers the door and looks delighted. "Nice to see you again! I'll let Ty know you're here . . . or did you come for Marius?" Her face falls a little.

Oh no. This is my second time asking to see Ty in a week after—well, *never* visiting him before. Does Mrs. Rivers think I *like* him?

And Marius is here? Bad enough I'm going to make Ty give

me what I want by threatening to tattle on him—now Marius will end up involved.

Mrs. Rivers leads me upstairs. "I have a question about homework," I explain, not wanting to give the poor woman the wrong idea.

"Boys!" Mrs. Rivers calls ahead. "Jadie is here. *To see Ty.*"

I groan silently. No wonder Ty wanted to meet at the playground last night.

"Boys?" Ty's mother pushes on his bedroom door, and it swings open. "Are you in there?" His mother glances back at me with embarrassment. "I guess they went out."

I peer past Mrs. Rivers, and what I see makes me straighten up like a trained hunting dog. That signal injector thingy is lying on Ty's desk next to his shark-in-a-jar. "There's the book I want," I say, pointing randomly. "If it's okay, I'll copy the questions I need."

"Sure." Mrs. Rivers looks disappointed that I won't be seeing her son.

"Thanks." I walk into the room and sit down at Ty's desk. "I'll just be a minute."

"Take your time," she says, backing away.

I don't think I have much time. Ty and Marius have probably gone off on an unauthorized 4-space adventure and might be back any second. The computer screen is awake; they haven't been gone long. I grab the signaling device, but that isn't all I need.

Calling up the start menu on Ty's laptop, I click on Recent Items and select an Excel spreadsheet. It isn't the one listing his course correction numbers, so I close it and try another. While this one opens, I glance around uneasily. Besides the fact that Ty and Marius could show up without warning, I'm worried about the Seers. Ty claims they aren't monitoring Agents closely, but they knew enough to calculate another way to destroy Sam's laptop, even after I reported Alia's course correction complete.

I look over my shoulder at Ty's closed closet door. The center is made of slatted wooden planks, and for some reason, the door gives off a creepy vibe. I'm tempted to cross the room and throw it open. But that's silly. If the Seers are spying on me, they're doing it somewhere kata from Earth, not from inside Ty's closet.

I turn back to the computer. This time, I've got the right file. Ty has the coordinates labeled in his spreadsheet next to the address of the Philadelphia sandwich shop and the note: *approx 30 feet from here, in an alley.* He's a precise evil mastermind, I'll give him that. Taking out my phone, I snap a picture of the whole sheet.

Go subterranean, huh? Thank you, Alia! This is much

better than my blackmail plan. Mrs. Rivers will tell Ty I was here and he'll guess what I've done, but there's nothing he can do about it.

I bolt from his chair and out of the room. Honestly, it was almost too easy.

13. TY

As soon as Jadie is gone, Ty slides open the closet door. Before he can step out, Marius pushes past him and sucks in a lungful of air. "Don't you ever do your laundry?"

"Quit overreacting."

"No, seriously. What's in there? A hundred unwashed gym socks?"

Ty sniffs discreetly. It is a bit ripe. But he shuts the closet door, leaving his dirty laundry for another day. "I never would've guessed your sister had the guts."

"For a second, I thought she was gonna catch us. It looked like she knew we were in the closet."

Hiding had been an impulse when Ty's mother called out that Jadie was here. He dragged a protesting Marius into the closet, and together they watched Jadie search his computer and steal the signal injector.

A lucky break. Now Ty doesn't have to figure out a way to give her the device without rousing her suspicions.

"What do we do next?" Marius asks.

"I put a radio transmitter inside that signal injector that'll alert us whenever the optics code is activated." Seeing the lack of comprehension on his friend's face, Ty elaborates. "We'll be able to tell when she calls the Transporter. It'll light up the button on this receiver." Opening a drawer in his desk, Ty removes a black box with one LED light and hands it to Marius. "Then we follow her."

"How?"

Ty digs into the drawer again and locates another signal injector. "I have more than one."

"No," says Marius. "I mean, how will we know where she goes?"

"She'll go back to the apartment where she had her course correction, or the street where I had mine. She's got some connection to that place—and that boy." For Jadie to defy the Seers, it has to be important...or personal. "Jadie was an abandoned baby. Could she have been from Philadelphia?"

"I dunno," Marius says with a shrug. "Nobody knows."

"Your parents didn't check where they found her?"

"Or me either."

Ty rolls his eyes. "The first thing I do on *any* course correction is find out where I am. I don't understand why nobody else is curious."

"Maybe my parents were too busy saving babies at the time. Geez, Ty."

In the case of rescuing Marius from a burning building, he has a point, but picking baby Jadie out of a snowbank wouldn't have required an urgent departure. Even twelve years ago, the Martins should have had cell phones with a basic map function. It would have taken seconds to determine where they were. The adult Agents seem to be so in love with "saving the world" they never deviate from their training: *Plug in the coordinates. Complete your mission. Leave immediately.*

Marius turns the receiver over in his hands, but he's not really looking at it. "What if Jadie did come from Philadelphia? What does that mean?"

"She's probably trying to figure out who she really is. Maybe that boy is related to her."

"What makes you think that?"

"Something made her defy my course correction, and she's fixated on one of hers, in the same location. Maybe she thinks she's found her family. She doesn't have to be right."

"She's searching for her birth family?" Marius looks like he's been sucker-punched in the stomach. "Why would she do that, after what they did to her? Why would she *want* to when she has *us*?"

Ha, a crack in the Wonderful Martin Family! Ty stifles his selfish glee for an even more selfish reason. He's always viewed the Martins' happiness with both disdain and envy, but he doesn't want Marius to know that. Marius is his friend, his partner in crime, the Watson to his Sherlock. Everyone knows Sherlock

Holmes was a miserable, unpleasant old fart. It's only Dr. Watson who makes the stories tolerable.

Instead of stoking the fire, Ty placates him. "She's curious. We'll follow her and find out more."

"Why?"

"Why?" Ty repeats. "You're the one who was so worried about your sister. *She's acting weird. Something's wrong. We have to figure out what it is.* That's what you said."

"That's why *I* want to keep track of her. But why do you? You don't even like her."

The dislike started on Jadie's side, but Ty doesn't argue the point. "Something strange is going on, and I want to know what it is. If Jadie traced her birth family, it's because of a course correction. She had the Transporter coordinates for their apartment. If that kid is her brother—we don't know he is, but she might think so—what's important about his computer? I'm *sure* that was the point of the mission. You should have seen her dive for it."

Marius frowns. "I don't know what you're getting at."

"I've always suspected the Seers are up to something. They aren't 'guiding the human race toward a better future.' Nobody goes to this much trouble just to help people."

"Well, *you* probably wouldn't. But my dad says nobody goes to this much trouble without a good reason."

"Yeah, a good reason for *themselves*. This whole setup with the Agents and the Transporter benefits *them* somehow. And Jadie meeting her brother thanks to their course correction is weird and suspicious."

Marius scowls. "You just said we don't know if he *is* her brother."

Ty has a gut feeling he is. "Don't you want to know if the Seers are up to something different from what they're telling us?"

"Nah," Marius says. "I thought we were going to use the Transporter to travel wherever we wanted. Like the Super Bowl. Or the World Series. And, um, the Olympics..."

Ty rolls his eyes. Even with the miracle of instant transportation at his disposal, Marius can't think beyond his favorite sporting events. Ty is more interested in places like Fort Knox, although his research suggests that gold bullion is not very portable and would be difficult to exchange for spendable currency. Recently, he's concluded that he should stick to cash and jewelry, at least until he's amassed enough of a fortune to...

To what?

He hasn't decided yet. He has a recurring fantasy where his father dangles over a shark tank in the hollowed-out interior of a volcano on a private island. Dr. Rivers is saying, "Okay, son. *Now* I respect you."

In his imagination, Ty is pressing the button to drop Dear Old Dad in the tank. Meanwhile Marius comes up with a few non-sports-related destinations. "The Eiffel Tower...the pyramids in Egypt...the Great Wall of China—"

"Sure," Ty interrupts. "We can tour the Seven Wonders of the World. Let's forget about Jadie and concentrate on cracking the Transporter code." He holds out a hand. "Give me the receiver back."

Marius clutches the box to his chest. "Well, I didn't mean *that*. It's my job to look out for her. I'm her brother, not some kid in Philadelphia. But I don't think this has anything to do with the Seers."

Even though it was a course correction that sent Jadie on a collision path with her possible family member and, it seems, his computer? Even though it was because of the Seers that Jadie survived as a baby and ended up becoming an Agent?

Ty sighs. If Marius wants to stick his head in the sand like an ostrich, fine. For now. But Ty intends to find out everything he can about the Seers and how they might be manipulating Jadie. Not for Jadie's sake, but his own. If he ever gets caught using the Transporter illicitly, he'll have a bargaining chip in his back pocket.

To Marius, Ty says, "Sure. We'll find out what Jadie's up to, make sure she's okay, and go back to working on the Transporter's coordinate system."

Marius visibly relaxes, and Ty marvels at his gullibility.

14. JADIE

It doesn't take me long to figure out how to use Ty's device.
I research on the internet what a signal injector does, then fire
the thing into my bracelet until I hit the right spot.

Every day for almost a week, I travel to that alley in Philadelphia and stand on that street, staring at the apartment
building next to the sandwich shop and hoping to see one of
the Lowells. I go at different times—times when I won't be
missed at home—but I don't see anyone who looks familiar.

That week, I get no course corrections. With no explanation.

We usually get one every day. The silence of my bracelet
haunts me. What do the Seers know? If they're angry with
me, why hasn't Miss Rose said something?

The stress gets to me. I forget to turn in an important science paper. I screw up in soccer practice and miss an easy
pass during a game. Coach pulls me aside to ask if there are
problems at home. I deny it, but I'm not sure she believes me.

When my secret trips to Philadelphia fail one after the
other, I consider using the original set of coordinates, the
ones for Sam's room. If I do it in the middle of the night, I can
sneak out to the living room and look for more information

about the family. If Sam wakes up, or if one of the parents is up late, I can hit the button and be extracted immediately. They'd get only the briefest glimpse of me. A ghost.

But I can't do that. It would be horrible to haunt the Lowells with the "ghost" of J.D.

Spring break starts, for school and soccer, leaving me more time to sneak off. Mom has to work, and so does Dad, because his college has its break on a different week. Alia's family leaves on vacation, so I can't get any more "gaming" advice from her. My other friends are either away or busy with their families, not that I can ask for their help anyway. Even Marius makes himself scarce—which probably means he and Ty are up to something.

Ty *must* know I stole his signal injector. But he hasn't said anything. Every time he sees me, he gives me a thin, unfriendly smile. I *think* that means he knows what I've done but can't do anything about it, just like I counted on.

Good. You do your secret stuff, and I'll do mine.

It isn't until one week after the day I took the Transporter with Ty that I see Sam again. It's around quarter to eight in Philadelphia, like before, and he's carrying his laptop again. I want to pull out my hair when I see it. I never take my laptop out of my house. Why doesn't he carry a thumb drive instead?

When he starts walking down the street, I follow him,

keeping half a block behind. Sam looks over his shoulder, and I almost bang my head on a lamppost ducking for cover. He turns a corner, and I hang back as long as I dare before trailing after him.

Four blocks later, he reaches his destination—a public library. I loiter on the corner while Sam limps up the stairs and through the glass doors. Then I take the stairs two at a time and peer through the glass before pulling a door open and walking into a vestibule.

"Why are you following me?"

I whirl around. Sam Lowell stares at me from a corner.

My cheeks flame. Getting caught is a rookie mistake.

Sam is tall enough that I have to tilt my head to look up at him. We have the same eyes, the same shape of nose, the same kinky curls in our hair. It's a connection I've never had with my own family. It rattles me, throwing me off my game.

Belatedly, I compose my face into a friendly but clueless expression. "What do you mean? I'm going to the library."

"No," Sam says firmly. "You followed me from my building. I saw you. A streetlamp isn't wide enough to hide a person."

Ouch.

"You're right. I followed you. Because . . . there's a game I play with my friends. How long can you follow someone before they notice? I earned four points, for four blocks."

This is the worst lie I've ever come up with. Something a seven-year-old might say. He's never going to buy it. *I'm dying here.*

"More like *one* point, for *one* block," Sam corrects me.

Okay, maybe Sam isn't up on the difference between seven- and thirteen-year-old girls. Wiping my sweaty hands on my jeans, I poise to run if this goes badly.

"What's your name?" he asks.

"Alia. What's yours?"

"Sam."

"Do you always take your laptop for walks after dinner? You dropped it last week. Maybe you should leave it at home."

"I don't plan to drop it again," he says indignantly. "I come here for the internet."

It takes me a few seconds to realize Sam means he doesn't have internet at home. For everyone I know, wireless internet in the house is a given. Like oxygen.

Sam's eyes dart around and end up focusing on my arms rather than my face. "This is going to sound strange, but *you* were the one following *me,* so . . . Would you do me a favor and roll up your sleeve?"

"What?" I say, like that's the weirdest request I've ever heard, but inside, my heart is racing. *He knows.*

"Last week, I saw something . . ." Sam's face twists in a

combination of pain and hopefulness. "On your arm. I want to see if I was imagining things—*please?*"

I hesitate, considering whether it's better to refuse outright or to comply and rely on my fail-safe plan. Weird request or not, he'll be suspicious if I refuse.

"You mean my birthmark?" I finally say, rolling up my sleeve. I've worn long sleeves on my visits this week, hoping to avoid this situation.

Sam draws in his breath. His eyes get wide, and he clutches his laptop tighter to his chest. "My sister had a birthmark exactly like that."

"Really? On her *right* arm?" In addition to the long sleeves, I took the precaution of reversing myself. "Are you sure?"

I watch Sam think about it. Then his shoulders slump, and he exhales. "No, on her left."

I nod. "Birthmarks like these are pretty common. That's what my doctor says. Hope I didn't freak you out."

"It's okay." The disappointment on his face hits me like a soccer ball to the stomach. "No problem." He turns, limping, toward the inner library door.

"What happened to your sister?" I call out.

Sam stops and gives me a look. "I didn't say anything happened to her."

"You said your sister *had* a birthmark like mine. So I'm

guessing something happened to her." After a second, I add, "I'm nosy."

"You sure are," Sam says. "We lost her."

"Sorry, but how do you lose a person?" My heart stops. I'm afraid he's going to tell me to mind my own business— that I'm going to get this close to an answer, only to have it snatched away.

"It was a carjacking. My mom stopped for a red light, and a guy opened the driver's door." Sam blinks, slowly, like he's trying to speak unemotionally. "He yanked her out of her seat. She fought him as hard as she could, but . . ." He trails off.

My mouth is dry, and my heart must've started again because now it's thumping like a kettledrum. "Did she get hurt?"

"Her coat got caught in the door, and she was dragged a few yards. If the guy hadn't cracked open the door to release her, she might've been killed. But she was okay." Sam heaves a big breath. "The guy drove away with J.D. in the backseat. She was only a baby. Police found the car two days later. They never found my sister."

"I'm sorry," I whisper.

"That's why I thought . . . when I saw your arm . . . maybe . . ." He shakes his head. "But it's the wrong arm." He's still staring at my birthmark, like he's stunned by the coincidence: a girl the right age, a mark the same shape and in the same position, but on the opposite arm.

"I'm sorry I remind you of your sister." I roll down my sleeve. "I'm sorry you thought you found her." This is a cruel trick.

"I didn't. Not really." That's a lie. Sam can barely wrench his eyes off my arm.

"What's wrong with your leg?" I blurt out.

Sam looks surprised, then laughs outright. "You're not shy, are you?"

"I told you I'm nosy." I might as well go all in. I can't come back here. It's cruel to these people, and it's not doing me any good either. If I want to know anything else, now's the time to ask, because this is going to be my last trip. It has to be.

"A hit-and-run driver clipped my bike six months ago," Sam says. "I fell, twisted my leg, and tore a ligament in my knee. The ACL, if you know what that is."

A wave of cold rolls down my body, like my blood is rushing toward my feet. I suspected his injury had something to do with the Seers. But *Dad* was the Agent who did it? And he told me the boy seemed fine.

"You okay?" Sam asks. "Wow, you got pale. Are you squeamish? You did ask."

I'm staring at his leg. "Does it hurt a lot? Tearing your ACL?"

"When I fell there was a snap, but it didn't hurt much. Wasn't until my knee wouldn't hold my weight—and it swelled up like a basketball—that I knew something was wrong."

My breath rushes out of me. Dad *thought* the boy was okay. He didn't lie. That part of my world is stable.

"Well . . . the library closes at nine, and there's a podcast I wanted to listen to." Sam tilts his head toward the inner doors of the library.

I've already pressed my luck. It's time to go. "Okay. See you around, maybe." With a cheery wave—which might be over-doing the goofy girl act—I turn and exit the library.

So now I know. My mother fought a carjacker for my sake, and my big brother still hopes I'll be found someday.

I also know the Seers are messing with the Lowell family. Over and over. Why? There's no hint that they're a crime family or terrorists. Whatever the Seers are trying to accomplish by wrecking their lives, *it's wrong.*

What can I do about it? Tell my parents? Confront Miss Rose?

I don't care about getting in trouble. But I worry what my parents will do when they discover they didn't *rescue* me—they stole me.

Walking into the first deserted alleyway I find, I hit the button on my bracelet. Being lifted into 4-space by the Transporter is so automatic, I don't give it a thought—until I stick my arm out for the port-lock and my bracelet doesn't latch in. Stumbling onto the platform, unanchored and off-balance, I grab for the console and miss because I reach for it with the wrong hand, forgetting I'm reversed. It's only luck that keeps me from pitching off the other side.

Once I have my feet solidly in the center of the platform, I knock my bracelet against the port-lock, but it won't latch.

Okay. Forget the port-lock. I press the Return button on the console. Nothing.

Ty said he thought our bracelets were strung on a four-dimensional fishing line. What if mine snapped? Nobody knows I'm out here. How am I going to get home?

Don't panic. Breathe, think, and then act. Play smart.

I take in a deep breath, stand up straight, and let the air out as I consider my options. I have just decided to enter the Philadelphia coordinates again and redo my request for pickup, when something invisible shoves me in the middle of my chest. I stagger backward, my right foot slipping off the platform.

That's when the abnormal gravity of this place catches me.

I don't fall like I would on Earth: 4-space whips me sideways in a dizzying arc and robs me of my breath before dropping me into an unfathomable universe.

15. SAM

Watching the girl leave, Sam regrets shooing her away. He enjoyed talking to her. But the disappointment of realizing she isn't J.D.—after a week of imagining she might be—is a blow.

Choosing a library table, he opens his laptop and connects to the Wi-Fi, his fingers moving listlessly through the steps. *You should've known it couldn't be her.*

He didn't get a good look at the girl's birthmark last week. He'd been humiliated by his fall and relieved to have his computer saved. After thanking the girl who caught it, he'd only spotted the mark on her arm as she ran off.

If he'd possessed two good legs, he would've chased her. Instead, he spent the next seven days in agonizing limbo. He watched for her every time he went outside, hoping that if she lived nearby, they'd cross paths. He said nothing to his parents. He couldn't get them riled up on the basis of a glimpse.

Inserting his earbuds, Sam tunes in to the podcast, although he's now lost interest.

His sister is almost certainly dead. What would a violent criminal do with a baby discovered in his possession? At the very least, he'd put her out of the vehicle. And it had been a cold, snowy day.

J.D.'s abduction was the worst thing that ever happened to his family, but there's no reason to be freshly upset about it now. It's an old, old wound.

While the host of the podcast introduces this week's topic, Sam opens the graphics program. His dad's formulas have given the software a new way to depict the geometric oddities of an Escher-type building, but there are still errors. He has two more weeks to turn in a working project, and if he can't meet that deadline, his teacher's friend will use a different landscape design. "We can circle back to your idea next year," the guy promised. But Sam's family needs the money now, not next year. He has to eliminate these flips, blank spots…reversals.

Sam sits up and freezes the program. Just now, one of the characters in his landscape walked up a set of stairs and turned, and the computer—glitching—flipped the image. Reversed it.

Sam stares at that reversed image on the computer screen.

To see such a similar birthmark on a girl the same age J.D. would've been—a girl with the same golden-brown hair J.D. had—is improbable. To have it be an almost-identical reversal…

What if I'm wrong?

Based on the photograph hanging in his living room, that birthmark was on J.D.'s left arm. What if the photograph is a reversal? He'll have to check against other pictures. But J.D.'s baby album is missing. Sam groans, rubbing his forehead. He can ask his parents. They'll remember for sure.

What outcome does he expect, realistically? That his father will say J.D.'s birthmark was really on her right arm? And then Sam will tell his parents that he's found her—that she's living somewhere nearby under the name Alia? Ridiculous!

But she followed me, not the other way around. After a week of Sam looking for her, the girl had found Sam and stalked him like a spy in a bad movie. What if she suspects something too? She asked what happened to my sister. Why did Sam let her go? He should've asked where she lived and who her parents were.

This is more than a coincidence, and I blew it!

Sam pounds a fist on the table, then looks up, realizing that two boys have stopped in front of him.

They're a couple of years younger than he is—middle school kids, like Alia. One is thin, white, and blond. The other, taller and Latino, scowls like he has a personal grudge against Sam. "What?" Sam asks.

The blond boy gestures at his own ears. Sam takes the hint and removes his earbuds. "What do you want?"

"This." The boy slaps Sam's laptop closed and snatches it off the table, earbuds trailing behind.

"Hey!" Sam launches to his feet.

The blond boy and his Latino friend both touch metal bracelets on their wrists. Their bodies contract into thin, smeared
lines and vanish.

Sam charges around the table as fast as his bad leg can carry
him, but there's no one to chase. No boys running away. No stolen computer to retrieve. The library is empty of other patrons,
and the librarian isn't at her desk.

No one but Sam has seen two boys disappear into thin air.

With his computer.

16. JADIE

My back slams against a solid surface, knocking the air from my body. The blow stuns me so much that it's a couple of seconds before I try to take a breath—and when I do, I fail. My lungs won't expand. I realize, with horror, that Miss Rose never told us whether there's oxygen in 4-space past the Transporter. Spots dance before my eyes.

Then my chest spasms and I suck in air. There *is* oxygen. My lungs *do* work. I had the wind knocked out of me. *A brief paralysis of the diaphragm,* was how Coach explained it to a girl who'd been hit in the chest with a ball. *You're okay. It only lasts a few seconds.*

I lie there for a minute, enjoying the sensation of breathing, but when I try to sit up, I panic again. Why can't I lift my arms and legs? Is my spine broken?

Gravity. I slide one arm backward and then the other until I can push my torso up and rest on my elbows. It takes every bit of strength I have. Gravity has pinned me like a rare-earth magnet on a steel plate.

In training, Miss Rose told us: "Gravity is a weak force in your braneworld."

"How so?" Ty asked. He was quick to challenge her.

"Drop something," she suggested.

Ty pushed a pencil off a table. It fell to the floor and rolled over next to Alia's feet. "Gravity. Works pretty good, in my opinion."

"But you can pick that pencil up without much effort." The smile on Miss Rose's avatar didn't waver. Well, it couldn't waver, no matter how much sass Ty gave her. Alia helpfully picked the pencil off the floor. "In my world," Miss Rose said, "counteracting gravity is not done without a great deal of energy."

Now I understand what she meant. I'm sweating by the time I make it to a sitting position. My body trembles like I'm lifting weights instead of holding my torso upright. When I move one hand to push the button on my bracelet, the sideways movement doesn't take as much effort. *Lateral motion is not as hard.* Unfortunately, the Transporter doesn't collect me.

There's one other button to try, the recessed one that summons Miss Rose. I press it with my fingernail and pray it works.

Lifting my chin to look up strains the muscles in my neck, but I want to see the platform I fell from. As always in 4-space, it's hard to identify anything. I see gray cylinders and sparkly strings in the ember-red sky—if it is a sky. A sheet of metal that's not the right color to be the platform juts out, and something made of magenta crystal hangs above me. But it's like that comparison with the pineapple. If you can't tell what a whole pineapple looks like from a tiny sliver, how can I tell what the platform looks like when my eyes have only seen a portion of it?

"Help!" I holler. "Is anyone out there?"

My voice vanishes into space. I'm a paper doll, making tiny paper noises. Who's listening, anyway? Ty claims there's no one out here, and considering the many unauthorized trips I've made in the past week, he's probably right.

That blow that knocked me off the platform—was it a broken piece of the Transporter? Did I accidentally land at a port-lock that's closed for repair?

Not only am I a paper doll in this world, I've fallen into malfunctioning machinery. Giving in to the gravity, I sink back onto the metal plate. *Stay still. Conserve energy. Wait for help.*

But is help coming? If my bracelet is broken and the call for Miss Rose doesn't work . . . My heart flutters. When Mom and Dad realize I'm gone, will they think to look for me in 4-space? I hate to think that might depend on Ty. If he hears I'm missing and guesses I ran into trouble out here, will he tell someone?

Suddenly, I realize I don't have to depend on Ty. *Marius* will figure it out and tell Mom and Dad. He may be Ty's partner in mischief, but he won't leave me stranded. I need to be patient. It'll take time for everyone to figure out where to look for me, but they'll get here eventually.

Patience isn't my strongest quality. Lying on the slab of metal, I poke at the buttons on my bracelet, over and over, just in case they start working. I yell "Help!" until my throat is sore. I stare into 4-space, hoping to see activity—specifically, someone coming to rescue me. But the only thing out here that moves is that magenta crystal above me, which shrinks and expands mysteriously.

Then, from somewhere closer to my level, red, glowing lights flicker, winking in and out, followed by a snuffling sound. I open my mouth to shout for help . . . and stop. Because what I'm hearing sounds more like wet, snotty breathing than the approach of a search party. And those glowing red lights look a bit like predator eyes peering out of the gloom.

The snorting grows louder, echoing so that I can't tell exactly where it's coming from. I swing my head back and forth, searching. Without warning, a black, twitching mound appears near my right elbow before morphing into a parade of sharp, jagged teeth—each one half as large as my body. I scream, instinct spurring my muscles into lifting my body—to stand, to run—but 4-space gravity slams me back down.

Thankfully, Jadie 2.0 takes over, snapping quick, logical thoughts into my brain. *Lateral movement doesn't fight the gravity.* Instead of trying to get up, I slither sideways. Something wet touches my hand, wrenching another scream from me. My fear excites the creature. Its snuffling speeds up, and it releases a cloud of hot, rancid breath. This time, I scream on purpose, trying to sound fierce and dangerous. When I spot a glimpse of gray fur, I ball up my fist and swing it sideways, thumping a hairy body.

The thing squeaks and slides away from me, vanishing kata or ana, where I can't see it. As much as I want to squeal like a five-year-old—I'm pretty sure I punched a giant four-dimensional rat—I hold myself still and alert. I can't spare the brainpower to fall apart because this thing hasn't gone far. I smell it.

Squirming sideways and fighting gravity isn't going to help—it's too big and I can't move fast enough—but aggression might. I need this thing to think I'm too strange, too loud, too scary. So I roar from my chest like a bear.

A blow from an unexpected direction cuts me off midhowl and rolls my body over. Now my face is pressed against the metal plate, a weight on my back in addition to the gravity pinning me down. Slimy drops of liquid slither down my face, pooling near my nose. Huge incisors loom in close, bringing a wave of rancid breath.

I scream, anticipating the bite, the crunch, *the end.*

Then a feathery touch sweeps across my shoulders, swiping the weight off my back as if it were nothing. The creature squawks in frustration.

A booming voice calls out, curling and echoing.

"Jaaaa-dieeeeee? Jaaaa-dieeee Maaaarrrr-tiiiiinnn?"

17. JADIE

Six huge, sepia-colored tubes appear in midair, swooping toward me.

I shriek and wiggle sideways to escape them.

A huge eye—all blue iris with no white around it and a horizontal slit for a pupil—looms above. "Jadie, it is Miss Rose. Be still."

I almost cry in relief and let my body go limp. The six tubes elongate as they tighten around me. *Six fingers?* Pressure around my torso pries me off the metal plate. Unidentifiable shapes sail past. Then, trees and buildings and a familiar bike trail. My feet hit the ground. A huge magenta crystal appears in front of me right before the six huge fingers let go and tunnel backward, out of existence. The last I glimpse of the real Miss Rose is half a dozen pink talons on the ends of those fingers.

I'm standing on a lighted path near the edge of my housing development, a short walk from home. If there were people around, I would throw myself at them and hug them, no matter who they were, but there's no one in sight. Instead I cross my arms and rock back and forth, marveling at the beauty of three-dimensional objects that make sense to my eyes and brain. *Hello, walking path! Hello, clouds! Hello, abandoned golf ball!*

"Jadie."

I turn around and jump backward. Miss Rose is standing there.

Not the four-dimensional Miss Rose who rescued me and placed me back in 3-space. Her avatar.

The three-dimensional stand-in for Miss Rose resembles a smartly dressed talk show host. Her hair is silver blond, styled to perfection. Her skin is a golden sepia, and her eyes are blue—the same shade as the huge eye I saw in 4-space—but the avatar has humanlike, round pupils in an iris surrounded by white.

My gaze drops to Miss Rose's hands, double-checking the number of fingers. Five, of course—one adorned by a large magenta ring.

"Are you hurt?" Miss Rose asks. The avatar's mouth doesn't move.

"No, I'm okay. Thank you for bringing me back." I unfold my arms and drop them to my sides. I might be craving a comforting hug, but I'm not going to get it from this avatar. And in spite of Miss Rose rescuing me, I don't want one from her.

The real Miss Rose is huge enough to pick me up with her six fingers.

"I am sorry this happened." Miss Rose can't change that fixed smile, but she does try to make her voice sound sympathetic. "I was not aware you were on the schedule for a course correction tonight."

"I, um . . ."

"I do not know why your bracelet malfunctioned," Miss Rose continues without waiting for my answer. "Its communication with the Transporter has somehow been severed. *This was a terrible mistake.* There are procedures to be followed, *and the consequences of ignoring them are dangerous.*" The tone of her voice shifts, from apologetic and concerned to something more harsh. "You were lucky I came across you when I did."

"Were you looking for me?"

"No. The bracelet is not functioning, and no one knew *you were not where you were supposed to be.* It was only by chance that I spotted you. As you must realize, in 4-space you are *very small and insubstantial.* I hate to think what might have happened . . ."

I shudder. "That rat thing . . . what was it?"

"The meeker? A prolific pest in my world. Like cockroaches in yours. They are *everywhere* in 4-space. Now go home and rest. This must have been terrifying for you. Put your bracelet on my avatar, and I will take it to be repaired. A working one will be delivered to you, and the Seers will make sure *this does not happen again.*"

With trembling fingers, I open my bracelet and fasten it around the cold and unresponsive wrist of the avatar. Its fingernails, I notice, are painted baby pink, just like the talons on Miss Rose's real hand. The color complements the magenta gemstone in her ring. Very fashionable for a four-dimensional lady.

Except, after glimpsing that enormous eye and those talons, I can't think of her as a lady. More like a giant monster. Mumbling "Thank you," I start to walk away.

"Oh, and Jadie," Miss Rose says. I stop and look back. "I unreversed you when I brought you back. Try not to be so foolish in the future."

"Sorry." I push back the sleeve on my left arm, checking for my birthmark. When I look up again, Miss Rose's avatar has vanished, taking my bracelet, her false smile, and that magenta-colored ring with her.

That ring. I shudder uncontrollably.

I am *positive* the huge crystal I saw when Miss Rose set me down on Earth was a sliver of that ring, or whatever that ring translates to in 4-space. But more importantly, it's also the same crystal I saw hovering above me after I fell off the Transporter platform.

Or was pushed off.

Miss Rose was there all along, watching me struggle with gravity, listening to me call for help, letting that meeker—*a furry cockroach with teeth?*—come close to chewing my face off before intervening. Her apology—with those carefully emphasized phrases—wasn't an apology at all. It was a warning.

Miss Rose wanted to make me see how *very small and insubstantial* I am. In her universe, I can be eaten by a cockroach.

The Seers know I've interfered with their plans for Sam Lowell, and Miss Rose just warned me to stay out of their business.

18. TY

Using a joystick connected to Sam's computer, Ty steers a human figure down a road curved like a Möbius strip. Distorted buildings line the street. Walking in a straight line eventually brings the virtual pedestrian back to its starting point.

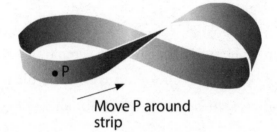

Move P around
strip

Marius peers over Ty's shoulder. "You think this program is important?"

"Gotta be. I've been through the whole hard drive. There's nothing else of interest on it. And this game... well, it's only the landscape for a game, but the graphics are unusual."

Ty switches his view to the coding behind the program. There's something *not right* about these lines of code, something in the math that shouldn't work. He traces his finger along one string of numbers, almost but not quite understanding what they mean.

Marius interrupts his train of thought. "What's so special about it? The crazy buildings? I've seen them before. He didn't invent them."

"Of course not." Ty rolls his stiff neck. "They're based on Escher drawings. But what this kid has done . . . What's his name again?"

"Sam Lowell," Marius snaps. "It's on those school assignments you looked through. Did you not pay attention?"

Ty glances up. "What's eating you?"

"What's eating me?" Marius paces the length of the room. "Jadie's got another family!"

"You're jealous? Now, that's dumb." Ty returns his attention to the laptop screen. "She's curious. Wouldn't you be, if you found your birth family?"

"No."

"That's because you know they're probably dead."

"Harsh, dude."

"But true."

"If they're dead, they didn't abandon me on purpose. Her family left her by the side of the road. So why'd she track them down and tell them who she was?"

"You don't know she did."

"We saw her through the library doors," Marius insists. "Rolling up her sleeve to show that boy her birthmark."

Ty meant they don't know she tracked her family down, versus stumbling upon them by accident. But, whatever. Jadie's family loyalty is a sore subject for Marius.

Occasionally, Ty wonders what it would be like to have a sister of his own. Based on what he's observed of Jadie, he assumes she'd spend her time butting into his business. Telling him not to drop Dad in the shark tank and wanting to keep ponies on his secret island hideout. Blah, blah, blah.

Pointing at the computer, Ty turns the conversation back to its starting point. "*Anyway,* Sam has used a software program to make two-dimensional drawings seem like they have four dimensions. What's interesting is he's altered the original code with some really complex mathematics. I've never seen anything like it."

"Too hard for you? Never heard you say that before."

"It's *new* to me. Give me time." The challenge of mastering something difficult excites him, and he flashes a grin at Marius. "Either Sammy is a genius, or he knows someone who is."

"Great," Marius groans. "Jadie's other brother is a genius. So, you think the Seers want to stop him from inventing this game? Why? Because they have stock in Nintendo?"

"I don't think it's the game that's important. It's how he changed the program, especially the math he used." Ty jumps up. "I need to borrow my dad's camera."

"The one that cost two thousand dollars?" Marius asks. "He lets you use it?"

"I didn't say I was going to *ask.*"

When Ty returns to his room with his dad's new camera, Marius is staring at his phone in puzzlement. "Got a text from Jadie." He holds up the phone for Ty to see.

What r u doing with ty 2nite? DON'T go out to 4space!

See, this is the problem with sisters. Always sticking their noses in.

"Do you think she found out we stole Sam's computer?" Marius frowns. "She's got a lot of nerve telling me not to do what she's been doing all week." He starts typing. "I'm gonna say we're playing video games." He gets a reply within seconds. "She says good, and she'll explain later."

"She doesn't know about the computer. She's being bossy, like usual." Ty sits down at his desk. "First thing I'm going to do is copy this program onto my computer. Sam's is crappy and slow."

"And you're doing this *why?*"

"Because the Seers don't want Sam to have the program. And that makes *me* want it."

"You don't know that." Marius crosses his arms and leans

against a wall. "Maybe they want to smash his computer so he'll fail a big school project or lose a college application essay."

Ty pauses, hands hovering over the keyboard. Marius could be right. He hates it when Marius is right. Then he shakes his head. "No. It's too big a coincidence. This math deals with *dimensions*."

After queuing up the files to copy, Ty turns his attention to the camera settings.

"What's the camera for?" Marius asks.

"I want to try the program with a different set of graphics." The continuous drive should take the rapid-fire shots he needs for his purpose. He readies the camera and eyes up his bedroom, dividing it into manageable sections.

Marius watches him for a few seconds, then says, "Do you think Jadie's original parents didn't abandon her? I saw a show about the Lindbergh baby once. Charles Lindbergh's baby was kidnapped, and the kidnapper killed the little boy or maybe dropped him accidentally. Do you think somebody who wasn't her parents left Jadie in danger?"

"Ding, ding, ding! Give the boy his prize." Ty pans the first section of his room with the camera, holding down the shutter-release button.

"You already thought of that?"

"Right after she started going to Philadelphia, yeah."

"Then the Seers made a mistake."

Ty glances at Marius. "Welllll…"

"Like you said, they don't know everything, even if Miss Rose says they do. They don't know we've been using the Transporter."

That's true. If the Seers had any idea that Ty and Marius—and now Jadie—were hijacking their equipment, Miss Rose would've confronted them by now. But when it comes to Jadie and her birth family, Ty suspects the Seers know exactly what they're doing. He only wishes he could figure out what that is—and whether their plans have any value to him.

"I don't understand why you're taking pictures of your room," Marius complains.

"I'm gonna load them onto the computer and use Sam's program on them. Which will, hopefully, create a virtual reality version of my bedroom."

"How long will that take?"

"Couple of hours. Most of that will be the files copying."

"Ugh." Marius flings himself down on Ty's bed and opens a game on his phone.

It takes almost three hours. Uploading the photos proves more laborious than Ty counted on. While he types in the repetitive commands, he ponders the strange mathematics in the software code. Surely, it wasn't invented for this application. *What was its original purpose, why are the Seers trying to suppress it, and how does a teen from Philadelphia have access to it?*

Marius has long since dropped off to sleep when Ty admits to himself that he's done all he can with what he's got. His initial excitement has dwindled to a frustration that niggles like an itch in the middle of his back. Maddening. Unreachable.

He shakes Marius's shoulder. "Wake up, Drool Boy."

"Uhhh..." Marius wipes his face and sits up. "Do you have it working?"

"See for yourself," Ty says sourly.

Yawning, Marius uses the touch pad to explore the graphics. "So? It's your room in virtual reality. Even more boring than Sam's Escher world."

He's right. Ty's photo sets supplied the geography, and Sam's program compiled the information. But Ty didn't get what he wanted. "Nothing I photographed takes advantage of the advanced mathematics written into the program. I don't know how to acquire images from four-dimensional perspectives."

"What?" Marius squints at Ty. "Man, it's"—he checks his phone—"two in the morning. Can you keep it simple?"

"He means he cannot take photographs from ana and kata."

The voice is deep and booming and comes out of nowhere. Ty and Marius look at each other, then whirl around, seeking the speaker. Two curved silver horns erupt into existence in midair. They close around Dad's camera, slide backward, and disappear, taking the camera with them.

At that moment, Ty understands exactly how Sam Lowell felt when they stole his computer.

19. TY

High-pitched laughter fills the room. The camera swoops into view over Ty's head, pinched between those horns.

No—they're *giant claws*.

"Give that back!" Ty grabs for the camera, but it disappears before he can reach it and reappears in another corner of the room.

When he prepares to dive for it again, Marius catches him by the shoulders. "Don't give them the satisfaction."

Ty's hands shake in rage, but there's no use playing Monkey in the Middle with bullies from the fourth dimension. Swallowing fear of the punishment he'll face if this camera is damaged, he crosses his arms. "Enough games. Why don't you show yourselves?"

"No games," says the deep voice. "I am taking the photographs you could not." The camera clatters onto the desk next to Ty's computer. "Upload those." The voice thins out into something more human-sounding, and a man materializes in the room. Ty snatches up the camera, shoots the newcomer his nastiest glare, and starts plugging in cables.

Based on its utter stillness, the invading presence is an avatar.

But while Miss Rose's avatar resembles a businesswoman, this one looks like a hippie. He wears a bandanna, an untucked plaid shirt, khaki cargo shorts, and sandals. His legs are hairy.

Marius scowls. "You don't look the way I expected a Seer to look."

That annoying twitter echoes around the room, emanating from somewhere outside three-dimensional space, while the deeper voice speaks through the avatar. "I am not one of your Seers."

"We are the opposite of Seers," the high-pitched voice adds.

"*Opposed* to the Seers is more accurate," the avatar says.

Marius sidles over next to Ty. "Do you believe them?"

Ty stares at the computer screen. "Maybe. Because they just made this program work." Using the pointer on the screen, he explores the virtual bedroom. It's now possible to simultaneously view the top of Ty's desk and the contents of his desk drawer. They can see the outside and the inside of the closet at the same time. There's a virtual version of Marius and Ty, and when viewed from a certain angle, their organs and guts are visible.

Marius recoils. "Ugh!"

Ty quickly moves the pointer away, feeling nauseous.

"Yes, Tyler Rivers and Marius Martin," says the giggly voice. "On your kata and ana sides, you are quite transparent!"

"How do you know our names?" Ty demands, his voice shaking more than he likes. "And who are you, if you're not Seers?"

"We have been observing you," the avatar says, "whenever we can get close to your braneworld without being caught. Late and early hours are best. Rrhoessha does not work at those times."

"Who?" asks Marius.

"Miss Rose," Ty guesses.

"Correct. Now, the question of who we are is complicated. I could make up a name as pretentious as the Seers—the Resisters, perhaps—but it would be easier for you to call me Dave and my companion Steve."

"Tell us your real names, not some patronizing nickname." *Miss Rose* is a silly name. It irks Ty that even the adults call her that. Like she's their kindergarten teacher.

"Very well. My name is Dhaffyidhre, and the one who accompanies me is Shteffrynha."

The first name sounds like a sneeze and the second like hocking a loogie. "Dave and Steve it is," Marius declares.

Ty lets it pass. At least they don't want to be called Mr. Dave and Mr. Steve. "What do you mean by *Resisters*, and why do you have to sneak around Rose?"

"We want to help you," Dave replies. "It is forbidden for our species to interfere with the lives of lower-dimensional beings. But the beings you call Seers are powerful, and your braneworld is well hidden. Not many of our people know it exists, and it is not protected the way the others are. They can get away with it."

"The others?" Marius repeats, dumbfounded.

"Did you think yours was the only one? There are many."

Ty tries to wrap his head around the idea of multiple three-dimensional universes tucked away in corners of 4-space. Hidden inside 4-D garages and basements with tarps thrown over them to keep them out of sight. He can almost picture it.

"Why do the Seers mess with our world if it's against the law in your universe?" Marius asks. "What do they want?"

"I never believed it was for our benefit," Ty grumbles.

"Ego, money, prestige," says Dave. "In your world, there are endangered species, yes? Protected because they are close to extinction? This makes them more desirable to a certain type of person."

"Right," Ty agrees.

"Consider yourselves a unique and endangered species. These beings who pretend to be 'Seers' have the magnitude of wealth that leads to boredom unless they engage their peers in high-stakes games. Their interference in your world is a complex gambling enterprise. Can a presidential election be swayed by the outcome of the World Series? Does the position of a gate in Thailand determine whether or not a neighboring country declares war? You are a live video game."

Marius opens his mouth, shuts it, opens it again, but doesn't produce any words. Ty nods. This is what he's been thinking for a long time. Well, not this exact thing, which is more insulting and outrageous than he imagined. "You Resisters," he says, "you can't stop them?"

"In your world, have the rich ever been swayed by the concerns of the poor on behalf of those even poorer?" Neither Ty nor Marius bothers to answer. "We have risked our lives getting close to you," Dave continues, "thwarting your tormentors in every way we can. Right now, our goal is to help you complete something they have been trying to sabotage."

Marius points at the computer. "That program? Why?"

"He does not understand, does he?" Steve remarks in a sing-song voice, like he's talking about a toddler.

Irked by Steve's amusement, Ty looks at the computer screen—where the dirty laundry pile in his closet is visible from the kata direction—and the potential of this perspective dawns on him. "If we get this program to work with pictures taken in 4-space, humans will be able to see whole four-dimensional objects, not just cross-sections of them."

Marius furrows his brow. "You mean take photos in 4-space and download them onto a computer?"

"No," Ty says, reasoning it out. "We load this program onto a portable screen—say, a tablet we carry with us—and when it puts the images together, we'll be able to see in 4-space while we're out there."

"Yes," Dave agrees. "You will see the Transporter for what it is, our world, the Seers, Miss Rose...everything."

Ty practically drools at the idea. "You enhanced my simulation by taking ana and kata pictures of my room. Can you do the same in 4-space to make this whole thing work?"

"How useful is the program if it requires the assistance of a 4-space being?"

Duh. Of course.

"Then what's the big deal?" Marius asks. "Why are the Seers trying to sabotage a program that *almost* lets us see in 4-space?"

"The program needs adaptation," Dave explains. "The mathematics of multiple dimensions must be expanded and written into the code so you can view my universe in the three dimensions you understand and have the program predict and display what you cannot perceive. When I took pictures from the ana and kata directions, I did the work for the computer. You need a program that does not need my help."

"Okay." Ty grabs a pad of paper and a pencil. "Tell me what needs to be added."

"I am a Resister, not a mathematician," Dave says regretfully. "And I have limited knowledge of human computers. You need the help of the person who changed this program in the first place—and the person who calculated the equations."

"Sam Lowell," Marius growls from between his teeth. "Boy genius."

"And his father, Dr. Eli Lowell. The math is his theory." Dave's avatar turns to face Marius. "I believe *you* have the means to convince Sam and Eli Lowell to help us."

Marius looks down at himself, like they're referring to something he's got on his person.

"He means Jadie," Ty explains.

Enlightenment crosses Marius's face, then worry. "Now, wait a—"

Ty interrupts him. "Yes, we've got Jadie. Tell us what you want us to do."

20. JADIE

My bracelet is sitting on my nightstand when I wake up. Miss Rose must've reached into my room from 4-space to return it while I was asleep, which is both creepy and threatening.

Just a reminder of how powerful I am compared to you, Jadie my dear.

I snap it around my wrist, and immediately it beeps, displaying a mission. My first since throwing that lady's bag in the street almost two weeks ago.

After my terrifying experience in 4-space yesterday, I'm nervous pressing the button for pickup, but everything works the way it usually does. My bracelet clicks into a port-lock, my platform rotates through the Transporter's mysterious parts, and I'm deposited back on Earth.

I land in a cramped bathroom. The bathtub is half full of water from a trickle dribbling out of the faucet. It must've been running for hours to get this high. I look at the display on my bracelet screen.

Turn the water on full force.

Before I do that, I decide to figure out where I am.

The bathroom door opens to a one-room apartment: living room, bedroom, and kitchen combined in a space the size of my family room. It doesn't take long to find a stack of mail on a table near the front door.

I'm in Naples, Italy—my first international course correction. That I know of. I hate to admit it, but Ty was right. It was dumb not to be tracking my movements all along. Choosing what looks like an advertisement postcard that won't be missed, I copy the Transporter coordinates for this apartment next to the address and stuff it into my back pocket. Maybe I'll give the numbers to Ty; maybe I won't. I haven't decided.

Returning to the bathroom, I turn the knob next to the faucet. The trickle becomes a waterfall.

Beneath the rim of the tub is a hole to prevent accidental overflow, but it's too small to let the water out as fast as it's coming in. Soon, the torrent will spill over the edge and onto the floor. Since this apartment is—I check out the window—on the third floor, the forecast for the people below is *heavy rain*.

Do the Seers want to ruin this person's floor or wreck the ceiling of the neighbors below? Maybe it's a test for me, Agent Jadie Martin, to see if I'll go back to following the Seers' directions without question.

Well, I followed the directions, but I have plenty of questions.

Why did Miss Rose terrorize *me* when Ty is the one who learned how to summon the Transporter? Why did she go through the charade of knocking me into 4-space and threatening me while pretending to provide rescue? If the Seers were watching, why didn't they prevent me from meeting my brother Sam?

My eyes sting. Despite everything I've discovered, the Lowells are strangers. My brother is Marius. My parents are Darrien and Becca Martin. *They* are my family.

So why am I trying to handle this alone?

Water pours over the rim of the tub and onto the floor, but I don't care what happens here anymore. I hit the button for transport.

The machine drops me off in my bedroom, and I hurry downstairs to find Mom alone in the kitchen, cooking eggs. "Where is everybody?"

"Your dad left for work early, and Marius slept over at Ty's."

It bothers me that Marius spent the night at Ty's house. I texted him, warning him not to go to 4-space, but he didn't make any promises.

While I help myself to a bowl of Cheerios, Mom asks, "Did

you have a course correction this morning? I checked on you, and you weren't there."

"Just got back."

My mother lifts the pot off the stove and carries it to the sink, where she pours off the water while carefully retaining the eggs in the pot.

"That's a whole lot of eggs," I mention, my mouth full of cereal.

"I'm making deviled eggs for a baby shower at the history department this afternoon."

That's my mom.

Mrs. Lowell may be my biological mother, but she's not *my mom*. Mom works fifteen hours a week as a bookkeeper and spends the rest of her time driving me and Marius wherever we need to go, running fundraisers for the PTA, and providing tasty treats for office parties at Dad's college. In between, she pops off to locations around the world, performing course corrections designed to save humankind.

At least that's what she thinks she's doing.

I'm going to have to tell her the truth. It'll break her heart—and it might put her in danger. Those pink talons slipped into my bedroom to lay a bracelet on my nightstand while I slept. What else would they do?

"Jadie, I'd like to talk to you about something."

She steals the words right out of my mouth! I stare at her while she deposits the boiled eggs on a towel and tests how hot they are with her fingertips. "Your dad said you were having trouble with your course corrections. Seeing the point of them."

No. I see the point too clearly: Sabotage the Lowell family in every way possible.

"I want to ask Miss Rose to do for you—and for all the kids—what she did for us. Take you on a course correction and show you the steps that lead to the desired outcome." Mom taps an egg on the counter before rolling it between her hands and sweeping back the shell with her thumb. "That's how *we* were convinced. Miss Rose should understand that younger Agents need the same reassurance."

What I'm thinking is: *Miss Rose can make up anything she wants, and we'll have no way to dispute her.* But what I say is: "Maybe she can use us to stop a mass shooting. From what I saw on the news, the last one could've been prevented if someone had removed the jam he put in the security door." Pushing my empty bowl aside, I reach for an egg to peel. "Of course, I'm only human. The Seers could have found a more complicated way to stop him."

Mom raises an eyebrow at my sarcasm. "Some things *need* to happen, Jadie. It guts me when I see those stories on the news and think: *We could have stopped that.* But the fact is, the Seers work toward the good for the maximum number of people, and some tragic events turn the course of history. Take the Triangle Shirtwaist Factory fire. It changed public opinion on labor laws."

Well, that's great. Except for everyone who died in the fire.

"But some of our course corrections could have bad results. Like what I did today might cause someone to flip out and commit the next horrible news story." Mom presses her lips together and doesn't answer. "Right?" I press her.

"Yes, baby. That's true."

The cereal turns to rocks in my stomach.

Mom goes on. "But you need to have faith that in the end . . ."

"Why should I have faith? Why should I believe Miss Rose?"

This time both eyebrows rise. "Miss Rose has been good to us. She tries to make sure her Agents want for nothing. But . . . I . . . *did* want for something I was lacking."

My spine curls. I know what Mom's going to say next.

"I couldn't have children." She makes it sound casual while she rolls another egg between her palms, but I hear the pain behind her words. "I saw lots of doctors, went through tests, but there was no fixing it. Then the Seers brought you into my life." She looks up at me, her eyes glistening. "I owe them my daughter and my son, beautiful, intelligent children who would have died without their intervention. Children who are destined to do great things in the service of mankind's future."

There it is. Why she trusts them.

I stare at the gouged and misshapen egg in my hand and try to consider the big picture. What if the Seers do bad things to the Lowells not because the Lowells are bad people, but because their suffering is good for mankind? Like, the hardships in Sam's life cause him to join the Peace Corps and . . .

I stop right there. If this were true, Miss Rose would've pulled me aside when she caught me interfering. She would've *explained*. Instead, she broke my bracelet, pushed me off the Transporter, and watched me fight a furry cockroach for my life.

When I raise my eyes to Mom, I'm sure they're as teary as hers.

"Have I helped?" she asks.

"Yes," I say truthfully. "There's something I need to show you."

"What, honey?"

"I'll be right back." I slip off the stool, out of the kitchen, and upstairs.

Jocelyn Dakota's baby book is hidden under my bed. I pull

it out and hesitate. This will devastate Mom. Once she sees it, everything will change.

I don't want my family to change.

But Mom needs to know what Miss Rose is capable of. Tightening my hands around the album, I run out of my bedroom . . .

. . . and straight into Marius, who's coming up the stairs.

We collide. Marius grabs the album to catch his balance.

"What are you doing?" he asks.

"Nothing. Going to see Mom." I try to move around him, but he blocks my path.

"With this?" He looks at the album. "Geez, Jadie. Are you really going to tell her about your other family?"

21. JADIE

While Marius explains what he knows and how he knows it, I shake my head, blindsided. "You *followed* me? Both of you?"

Standing there, on the upstairs landing, I feel almost as unbalanced as I did in the Lowells' living room, staring at their family portrait. It's not as earth-shattering, but still a shock to learn that Marius and Ty were spying on me when I stole the signal injector. That they tracked my use of it and followed me. Every. Single. Time. Anger and embarrassment wrestle in my gut.

"We traveled about five minutes behind you," Marius says. "As soon as we landed, we'd go the opposite direction from the way we knew you'd go, then around the block to watch you from a distance."

Embarrassment wins.

He points at J.D.'s album. "You can't show that to Mom. She'll freak out. And we're nothing but a game to the Seers. Who knows what they might do to 'correct' the situation!"

"What d'you mean '*we're nothing but a game*'?"

"Me and Ty met some 4-space—uh, *people*? Not Seers.

Listen, you can't say anything to Mom about finding your real family. She'll run right to Miss Rose, and that'll be a disaster."

"Jadie?" Mom calls from the hallway downstairs.

Marius and I stare at each other, and he shifts his body to block her view of the album. "Oh, Marius, you're home," she says, looking up and spotting him. "Good. Your chores await. And, Jadie, I just received a course correction. Is it okay if we finish our talk later?"

I glance at my brother. "Sure, Mom."

Mom hurries off toward the laundry room, her designated launching point. As soon as she's gone, Marius yanks the photo album out of my hands. He marches into my room, sets it on my desk, and opens it. He doesn't ask permission, but it's a relief to share the burden.

Turning pages, he scans the photos. "Huh. They don't look like people who abandon babies in the snow."

"They didn't. The guy who hijacked their car did that."

Marius nods grimly. "Like the Lindbergh baby."

"I don't think that was a carjacking, but yeah."

He glances sideways at me. "What did Sam say when you told him who you were?"

"What? I didn't tell him. Are you crazy?"

Marius shuts the album. "Jadie, I *saw* you through the glass door of the library. You showed him your birthmark."

I cross my arms, upset I didn't know he was there. "I was proving I *wasn't* his sister. I was reversed, dummy. He'd seen the mark on my last visit, and I had to convince him it was on the wrong arm. Why would I tell him the truth? He'd tell his parents, and they'd call the police!"

"You're not"—Marius's brow crumples—"trying to reunite with them?"

"No! They might be my birth family, but they're not my *real* family." I punch him in the arm. "You dingbat."

"Then why were you looking for them?"

"I found them by accident, and I wanted to know what happened—how I ended up by the side of the road." I sigh because now it's a lot more complicated. "That would've been all if I hadn't figured out that their family keeps getting targeted for course corrections. Sam was injured by a car that Dad sent into his path. *Our dad.*"

"What? How do you know that?"

"Dad mentioned it, but he didn't know the boy was my . . . was related to me. And there's more." I lower my voice. "After talking to Sam last night, I had an accident on the Transporter and was rescued by Miss Rose. Except it wasn't an accident. I think she's figured out what I know and is trying to scare me."

"Dave and Steve said the Seers would punish us if we

figured things out." Marius clenches both hands. "What *kind* of accident?"

Instead of answering, I push him into the chair beside my desk. "Who are Dave and Steve? Tell me that first."

I sit on the edge of my bed while I listen to his story. It contradicts everything I've been taught—and everything Mom said—but makes disturbing sense. "They said *gambling*? We're a *game* to them?"

"Yeah, our universe is Las Vegas, and Miss Rose is the lady who spins the roulette wheel. These new guys said that Sam Lowell was halfway to inventing something the Seers don't want made. On his computer."

"They've tried twice to wreck it."

Marius squirms in his chair. "Me and Ty stole it."

"What?!"

"We stole his computer. We followed you to the library, and when you left, we grabbed his computer."

"What the hell, Marius! Why'd you do that?"

"Ty wanted to know what was so important." Marius leans forward, his eyes locked on mine. "Sam's working on a program that can help humans see in 4-space. It's just a video game to him, but it might work for real. That's what the Seers don't want us to have—a way to see what's going on out there. If Sam finishes it . . . if we give it back to him and let him finish it . . . we'll be fighting them. That's what Dave and Steve said."

I gasp as it hits me. "The course correction is complete! The computer was stolen. It's as good as destroyed."

"But Dave said—"

"I don't care what Dave said. If the computer stays stolen, maybe the Seers will leave the Lowells alone." I don't know how the bike accident ties in with the computer, or what that has to do with giving baby J.D. to the Martins, but if their goal is for Sam to never finish this program, we can make that happen.

Marius shakes his head, not convinced. "Look," I say. "Sam knows nothing about the Seers, but his life has been messed up by them. He's not my brother the same way *you* are, but I feel responsible for him because I know what's going on. Do you get that?"

"Well . . ."

"Ty's an evil genius. Let *him* figure the program out. He's better equipped to handle whatever the Seers throw at him than Sam Lowell, don't you think?"

Marius sighs grudgingly. "You have a point."

"Tell him," I demand. "Tell Ty right now that we're leaving Sam alone." If Ty's as smart as he thinks, he'll take a hammer to Sam's computer and forget about it. The Seers are not the benevolent beings we believed them to be, and their minion Miss Rose could squish us between her six gigantic fingers.

Perhaps Marius is thinking the same thing, because he nods and takes out his phone.

Ty answers immediately. Marius puts the phone on speaker, and I hear Ty ask, "What'd she say?"

"She doesn't want Sam Lowell involved. She wants the Seers to consider the course correction complete so they'll leave his family alone."

"Okay," says Ty.

"Maybe it's not a good idea to mess with that program anyway. Maybe . . . uh, what'd you say?"

"Okay," Ty repeats. "I got it."

Marius and I look at each other in surprise. Neither of us expected Ty to give in that easily. "You're okay with that?" Marius asks.

"She doesn't want me to involve Sam in my plans," Ty says. "So I won't."

"Plans? What plans? Wait a minute—"

But Ty has already disconnected.

22. TY

Ty realized, not long after Marius left, that Sam Lowell was superfluous to his plans. Sam's only a programmer, and Ty can do that work as well as, if not better than, he can.

The person they need is Dr. Lowell. Jadie's biological father.

If Ty feels the slightest twinge when he proposes his idea to Dave—or when Dave enthusiastically devises a method for carrying it out—he brushes it off. It's not as if they're going to dangle the man over a shark tank. Ty names the plan Operation Captive Audience because that sounds so much better than kidnapping.

Dave completes the first phase that afternoon. When he returns for Ty, he doesn't bother inserting an avatar into the room, instead calling out from 4-space: "It is done. Are you ready?" Before Ty can respond, huge fingers clamp around his waist and yank him out of his universe.

He flies past the usual array of nonsensical, morphing shapes—cross-sections of the Transporter—but then he plunges into darkness, gripped around the middle by a hand larger than his entire body. It feels as if he's being carted around like a child's action figure. He bites back a protest only because he knows Dave has grabbed Dr. Lowell from under the noses of the Seers (if they have noses), and there's no time to demand a more dignified form of transport.

The darkness ends abruptly with Ty looking down into a strange white room. From his viewpoint in 4-space, the structure is foreshortened but cubeish in shape.

Inside, a scholarly-looking man with glasses and rumpled hair walks along one of the walls, examining it with his hands. He's wearing a suit, although the tie has been pulled loose, and he moves sluggishly, as though his shoes are mired in mud. The only other items in the room are a desk, a chair, and a rolling suitcase that Ty suspects came with their captive.

Dave drops Ty into the center of the room and plops his Resister avatar down as well.

Dr. Lowell, who was bending over to peer beneath the desk, straightens up and turns around. Although his visitors have appeared mysteriously in the blink of an eye, the scientist does not look frightened—perplexed, maybe, and indignant. "If this is an alien abduction, it's extremely clichéd, and—" He breaks off, seeming surprised by the four-dimensional twist in his voice.

Ty clears his throat. "Welcome to the fourth dimension, Dr. Lowell."

"Where am I?"

"Sound travels differently here, but you'll get used to it. I'll repeat. This is—"

"I understood what you said," Dr. Lowell interrupts. "But I don't believe you." His expression is at odds with his words. Something sparks in his eyes, and he looks around the featureless white room with a new revelation.

"Dr. Lowell, you know where you are," Dave's avatar says without moving its mouth. "This is your life's work."

"Dimensional theory," Ty adds.

"I know what he means." Dr. Lowell points at Dave. "What is that? Some kind of simulacrum?"

"We call it an avatar, but *simulacrum* works too. He lives in 4-space in his true form but uses this stand-in to interact with humans."

"Why am I here?"

"Because you are the best in your field and the only person who can help us," Dave says.

Dr. Lowell shakes his head. "My field is dead. I've been told that at every job interview for the past year."

"It was arranged for you to fail at your interviews."

"What? Who *are* you?"

"You can call me Dave," the avatar says. "And this is Tyler. We have brought you here to give you firsthand knowledge of the fourth spatial dimension so that you can complete your unified theory of physics."

"Why don't you save a lot of time and *give* me the completed theory?" Dr. Lowell turns toward the desk and, when he sees what's on it, laughs shortly. "I see. You don't *have* a theory."

Dave replies in a slightly insulted tone. "I know what goes into it. But only you can do the mathematical calculations."

On the desk are several pads of lined paper, pencils, and a slide rule. Dr. Lowell picks up the slide rule, which stubbornly resists, like a magnet, even though the desk is made of wood. "You don't need to provide me with something as advanced as this. Don't you have an *abacus* I can use?"

Ty laughs in spite of himself. He doesn't want to like this man—he's nothing but a means to an end—but Ty has to admit that Dr. Lowell is handling the situation with the poise and sarcastic humor of...well...Jadie. "He has a point, Dave. Can't we give him a computer?"

"A computer will not work in this containment unit," Dave says. "This room is a tesseract, Dr. Lowell. Are you familiar with that term? A tesseract is a four-dimensional version of a cube."

"I know what a tesseract is," the scientist snaps. "The light source is coming from a part of the room I can't see. The kata side, perhaps? That's why there aren't any shadows under the desk."

Ty stoops and looks. Dr. Lowell is right. There are no shadows.

"The light is on the ana side," Dave explains. "Shadows are thrown in the kata direction, where you cannot see them.

Currently, this tesseract is subjected to forces that counteract gravity in a way similar to centrifugal force on your world."

"*Counteract* gravity?" Dr. Lowell lifts one foot off the floor like he's pulling up a suction cup.

"Yes. That is a *diminished* version of our gravity. If you were subjected to the full effect, you would be incapacitated. It is like whirling a bucket of water in a circle with a rope in your world. The water will defy gravity and stay contained within the bucket. Consider this room the bucket; it is moving through our space at a high rate of speed, lessening the effect of our gravity."

"Lessening but not overcoming." Dr. Lowell drops the slide rule, and it is slapped to the desk as if by an invisible flyswatter.

"Gravity acts as a wave moving through different dimensions. 4-space experiences the apex of the wave, the highest magnitude of gravity. 3-space enjoys the nadir, its bottommost and weakest point. In our universe, gravity is an overwhelming, inhibiting reality that supersedes all others. In yours, it simply keeps planets revolving around suns and causes objects to fall to the ground."

Under other circumstances, this would be fascinating, but Ty turns the subject back to the purpose of the enterprise. "Why can't he have a computer in here, Dave?"

"Electronics are disrupted inside the tesseract."

Dr. Lowell screws up his face, as if Dave has said something silly. But Ty focuses on the *problem*. "We can't fix the program if electronics don't work here."

Dave replies calmly. "You said you could complete the program at home, given the correct mathematics."

That is *not* what they discussed earlier.

"Tyler, how did you come to be here?" Dr. Lowell speaks gently to him. "Were you abducted like I was?"

"I'm here by choice."

"Where's your family?" the scientist presses. "Do you have one?"

Ty's irritation flashes. "They're at home."

"Then you'll understand how important it is that I get back to my wife and my son. I'll accept a tour of four-dimensional space, if that's what's on offer, but I'll do the calculations at home."

"That is not possible," Dave says. "I am not the only four-dimensional being keeping an eye on you. If we send you back to Earth, the others will know. And they do not want a unified theory developed."

"But I can *think* better if I'm not worried about my family." Dr. Lowell waves a hand at the stark white cubicle. "Frankly, I can't work under these conditions."

He's lying. His eyes keep returning to the pad of paper and pencil. Ty gets the impression Dr. Lowell can barely restrain himself from diving into that desk chair to record everything he's observed so far. Sure, he has to make a token protest…but Ty's father would abandon his family in a heartbeat for a career opportunity like the one Dave is offering. Ty has no doubt this man will do the same.

"Dr. Lowell." Ty uses what he hopes is a persuasive tone. "Enemies in the fourth dimension have tried to stop you from finishing your theory. You can't go home right now."

"I won't negotiate." The man crosses his arms. "If you don't put me back, I won't calculate so much as two plus two."

Now he's just being difficult. Ty opens his mouth to say something snippy, but Dave speaks first.

"We have not brought you here without an incentive. Complete the work on your theory, and we will reunite your family. You. Your wife. Your son. And your daughter."

"I don't have…" Dr. Lowell stops, then swallows hard. "I did have…" His eyes become glassy, moving from the lifeless avatar to Ty. "You can't mean…"

"Your missing daughter." Ty smirks. "Jocelyn Dakota—but we call her Jadie. I know her pretty well. Do what we ask, and we'll bring her back to you."

23. TY

Ty doesn't expect Dr. Lowell to drop to his knees and thank him, though he anticipates *some* degree of gratitude. Therefore, the depth of the man's anger catches him by surprise.

"Your cruelty is astounding," Dr. Lowell growls. "I know you're a child, so I'd like to think you don't understand the emotional impact of such a lie."

Ty throws his hands up in innocence. "I'm not lying! Here, I'll prove it." He pulls out his phone to share Jadie's seventh-grade school portrait and soccer team photos from last year's yearbook, snapped for this purpose.

But the phone is dead.

"Electronics do not work in this room," Dave reminds him.

Dr. Lowell shoots Dave's avatar a knowing glance before turning on Ty again. "Perhaps you've been lied to as well."

"No. Jadie was found by the side of the road when she was a baby, and since then she's been living with the family in the house next to mine. There's a birthmark over her left elbow *here*." Ty indicates the spot on his own arm.

Dr. Lowell's face remains rigid. "I want to believe you. But why should I? Why would you know my daughter? Who *are* you?"

"I'm someone whose life has been interfered with by 4-space beings, just like you. They call themselves the Seers, and they play with humans for entertainment."

"After your daughter was abducted," Dave says, "what happened to you, Dr. Lowell?"

The scientist turns his scowl on the avatar. "Why don't *you* tell *me*, since you seem to know everything about my life?"

"You did not start postgraduate classes when you were supposed to, and you lost your position in the doctoral program," Dave says. "It was eighteen months before you went back to get your doctorate. Your education was delayed."

"Do you think I cared about that? I lost my baby girl!"

"You didn't lose her, she was stolen," Ty reminds him. "By creatures who didn't want you studying dimensional theory."

"You got off easy," Dave says. "Your daughter was moved to a different family, by whom she has been well cared for ever since. You made it back to school, although every time you got close to producing a unified theory of physics, something happened to set you back."

"You call that getting off easy?"

"The last person who came as close as you have to the mathematical truths of the universe was *killed*, Dr, Lowell."

"What?" A feathery sensation runs up the back of Ty's neck. Dave never mentioned anyone getting killed.

"But you want *me* to complete the theory?" Dr. Lowell's eyes bounce off the avatar and wander across the ceiling and walls, seeking the real Dave. "So these unseen enemies will kill me too?" His wandering gaze lands on Ty like a laser beam, and Ty swallows uneasily.

"You are safe here, Dr. Lowell," Dave says in a placating voice. "I promise."

"Is my family safe? What happens when I've finished the work? You're not planning to keep me in this cage forever, are you?" Dr. Lowell takes off his glasses to clean them on his shirt, muttering under his breath. When he shoves them back on, he glares at the ceiling. "*Why* do you want me to finish the theory?"

"Your theory will provide the basis for a computer program that compiles images collected in three dimensions and postulates the appearance of the missing fourth dimension, allowing you to see an approximation of reality in 4-space."

"That sounds like..." Dr. Lowell trails off, as if having second thoughts about saying what pops into his mind.

"Sam's program?" Ty pipes up. "Yeah, I stole that from him. Took the whole computer, actually."

"You did *what?*"

"That means he's safe. Confused, but safe." Ty smirks again. "You're welcome."

Two fleshy tubes with protuberant knuckles plunge down

from the ceiling, causing Dr. Lowell to jump backward. Pinched between curved claws is a leather-bound journal with a worn cover. "This journal contains the remains of the last scientist's work." Dave deposits the book on the desk and withdraws his fingers from the room. "I believe you will find that his formulas reinforce your theories and take them one step further. Work quickly and fill in the gaps. Your absence will not go unnoticed. The beings who call themselves Seers will squabble among themselves, trying to figure out which one of them moved you and why. That will buy us time, but we need to get you and a completed theory back to your braneworld as soon as possible. We will help you disperse the unified theory worldwide, and Tyler will finish the program your son started."

"And then the 'Seers' will kill me," Dr. Lowell concludes, then looks at Ty. "And you too. Aren't you worried?"

Well, he wasn't before... "Dave?" *You never mentioned a dead physicist!*

"Rest assured. By their own code of honor, they can do nothing to interfere if your theory becomes widely known," Dave says.

"The code of honor of beings who stole my child?"

"Some of them will suffer a loss of status. Others will rise in their place. Scientific development in your braneworld will progress, and their game will change."

"And we'll have a program for seeing in 4-space, thanks to you," Ty adds pointedly. For a physicist whose wild theories are proving true, Dr. Lowell doesn't seem enthused. Even allowing for the captive audience scenario (okay, kidnapping), Ty thinks he'd be pretty excited if he were in Dr. Lowell's shoes.

"Fat lot of good that'll do," Dr. Lowell says curtly. "Not if electrons don't—"

Huge fingers grab Ty and lift him kata, out of the room. The white containment vessel that holds Dr. Lowell becomes visible as Dave moves away from it, and Ty's brain *almost* grasps what a tesseract looks like before it dwindles to a distant white point.

"What'd you do that for?" Ty demands. "What was Dr. Lowell saying about electrons?"

"He is angry and defiant, but that will not last." When he isn't speaking through the avatar, Dave's voice fills Ty's ears with its twisty, four-dimensional hugeness. "Left alone with nothing but that journal, he will work. To earn his freedom and regain his daughter."

Ty squirms. It's disconcerting to be held in the grasp of a being he can glimpse only in bits and pieces. Knobby, muscular flesh flexes in and out of sight. Thick black wires wriggle and bounce. "Why'd you yank me out of there? It doesn't make him trust us any better."

He's answered not by Dave's resounding voice, but by the high-pitched singsong of Steve. "Time to take Tyler home!"

"Shteffrynha signaled me that your absence has been noted," Dave says. "I must get you back to your braneworld, or the Seers will realize you are not hitching rides on their Transporter. Yes, Tyler, they know you use it without permission. I am sure many bets are placed on where you will go and what you will do. But if they suspect you are collaborating with someone from their world..."

"Can I go back and talk to the scientist?" Steve wheezes.

"Stay away from him," Dave's voice booms. "You will distract him from his work."

"You never let me have any fun." A wild, bulbous green eye with orange flecks and a horizontal black pupil swoops in close to Ty's head.

He flinches. The eyeball withdraws and then Ty sees nothing but dark stones, occasionally interrupted by a flickering red light. Filling in the blanks with his imagination, Ty thinks they might be passing through a tunnel lit by torches.

"You never told me the Seers killed a scientist to stop him from finishing his theory."

"The Seers send their Agents to perform many actions on Earth. Did you think none of them resulted in deaths? You are not that naïve, Tyler."

Truth is, he did suspect that some of the course corrections resulted in unhappy outcomes. He just never thought *he* might be in danger.

"Do not worry," Dave says. "Once you have developed the means for seeing into 4-space, the game will change for the Seers. Making your braneworld more aware of our world cheapens the experience for them. When it is no longer fun, they will move on to other games."

Ty's heart rate spikes. "What about the Transporter? If the Seers abandon us, they won't dismantle the machinery, will they?" Without the Transporter, a means of seeing in 4-space is useless to him.

"Their kind never cleans up their toys. The Transporter will stay, and we will give you the key to its coordinate system. As we promised."

Ty's mind races in anticipation of the future.

The Seers and Miss Rose—gone.

Pointless missions masquerading as course corrections—gone.

And Ty—left with the power of unlimited, instantaneous transportation. He can go anywhere he wants, whenever he wants. He'll never be trapped someplace he isn't wanted ever again.

Like here. Ty glimpses the roof line of his father's house right before plunging into his own bedroom. "Keep a low profile until I deliver Dr. Lowell's calculations," Dave's voice rumbles from 4-space. "No more unauthorized trips. We need you to complete the work quickly when the time comes, and it is better if the Seers do not find you interesting to watch."

"Got it," Ty agrees.

The last thing he needs is the Seers and Miss Rose mucking everything up when he's this close to getting what he wants.

24. JADIE

When I tell Marius I want to return the baby album to the Lowells, he says I'm nuts. "If Miss Rose pushed you off the Transporter for meeting Sam, what's she gonna do if you go back?"

"I took the album to learn the truth. I don't want to keep it. Besides, after you and Ty stole Sam's computer, the least I can do is give him back his sister's pictures."

"You know, it's weird how you talk about that baby like it's not you."

I shrug. That's the way I deal with it. Jadie Martin and J.D. Lowell have to stay two different people or my brain will explode.

Marius shakes his head in an exaggerated, doomed sort of way, the way he probably does with Ty. "What's your plan?"

"I'll use the coordinates given to Alia. That lands me in Sam's bedroom, so I'll have to do it in the middle of the night—like, around two a.m. I'll leave the album and go. Two seconds, tops."

"What if he's not asleep?"

"One second, then. He'll see a lot less of me than he saw of you when you stole his computer."

Marius crosses his arms over his chest. "I'm coming with you."

"I don't think that's a good idea."

Marius shakes his head. "I'm coming, and I'm coming prepared. If Miss Rose sics any furry cockroaches on you, they'll have to go through me first."

✳

It's cute that Marius wants to protect me, but this trip is a one-person job. So I tell him I'll wake him at two in the morning, but I set my alarm for one-forty-five, planning to leave and return before he wakes up.

But Marius is smarter than I think, because he shakes me awake at one-forty. "Let's go."

I sigh and roll out of bed fully dressed.

Marius is holding a backpack with a flashlight tucked into the outside mesh pocket. He opens it, revealing Mom's biggest chopping knife, a kitchen lighter, and the fireplace poker. "What, no nunchaku or throwing stars?" I ask.

"You won't be laughing when I fight the monsters off. D'you want to put the album inside?"

Unzipping the backpack to take it out will add seconds to

our mission, but I also don't want to drop the album if we encounter trouble in 4-space. I slip the album inside a separate compartment from the poker and the knife so their pointy parts won't tear the cover.

He shoulders the backpack, and we use the signal injector on each of our bracelets to call the Transporter. Seconds later, we're standing on adjacent platforms.

Marius peers through the metal grate between his feet. "How far did you fall?"

"I didn't break anything, so it couldn't have been far."

Marius grabs his flashlight and aims it through the grating. The light flares for a second and fades out. He clicks the button several times and knocks the battery case against the platform. "Should've checked the batteries," I say.

Marius shoves the flashlight back into its pocket with a frown. "I did check."

"You ready to go?" When he nods, I call out eleven of the digits in the coordinates, which we both enter into our consoles. "The last digit is a seven, but wait two seconds after I enter it, so I can step out of the way."

"Other way 'round. I'm going first." Before I can argue, Marius punches the seven, and his platform moves away from mine.

I spend my two seconds copying the gesture Homer Simpson makes when he thinks about strangling Bart. Then I press seven and follow my brother.

The lights are off in Sam's room when I arrive, but there's enough illumination from under the door to see that the bed is empty. Lights in the hallway are on, and we can hear loud voices arguing elsewhere in the apartment.

"They're awake. Let's get out of here," Marius hisses.

"Wait! We should leave the album."

Marius swings the backpack off his shoulder and unzips it. I cross the room in two strides, crack the door open, and listen.

"It took five hours for one of you to show up!" a woman is yelling. "Don't tell me to *calm down!*"

"Ma'am, this isn't helping..." A man's voice, dry and condescending.

"I hope you don't have to wait forty-eight hours to file a missing person report!"

"That's only on TV, ma'am. I'll file this as soon as I get back to the station."

"And then what?" I recognize Sam's voice. "What will you do to look for him?"

"Okay," Marius whispers, laying the album on Sam's desk. "Let's go."

I shake my head. "Something's wrong." He joins me at the door, and together we listen while the man asks if Mr. Lowell likes to hang out at bars or if he uses drugs.

"It's *Doctor* Lowell," the woman snaps. "And no. He does not."

"Medical doctor, is he?"

"No, a professor of physics."

"At what university?"

Mrs. Lowell pauses. "He's out of work right now."

"Un-em-ployed." The man—who must be a cop—drags out the word like he's writing it down. "That's too bad. He been depressed lately?"

"No—"

"Marital problems? Arguments over money?"

"Excuse me, Officer. That's not what's going on." I silently cheer when Sam interrupts the cop's insulting questions. "My dad was supposed to make a proposal at Rutgers University today. He left at noon to catch a train, and he never made it to his appointment. He's not depressed, and he's not out drinking. Something *happened* to him."

Marius and I exchange glances.

The cop clears his throat. "I can investigate whether he redeemed his train ticket—or traded it in for another destination."

I wrap my hand around Marius's arm and whisper, "You

took the laptop away from Sam like the Seers wanted. So what's this about?"

"Dave said Sam *and* his dad were important," Marius whispers back. "The Seers were out to stop both of them."

"You didn't tell me that!"

"I forgot!"

We listen through the crack in the door. The policeman is leaving. He promises to be in touch, with a total lack of interest in his voice.

But if the Seers did something to Sam's dad, the police can't help.

"I have to try to do something." I release my grip on Marius's arm. "You can go home if you don't want to be involved."

Marius doesn't pause to think it over. "I'm sticking with you."

After the cop leaves, Mrs. Lowell starts crying. We can't hear everything she and her son say to each other, but it twists my stomach into knots knowing how worried they must be. I'm worried too. Sam was hit by a car. What will the Seers do to his dad?

He's my dad too, but it's easier to accept Sam as a brother than to identify Dr. and Mrs. Lowell as parents.

Brother is an honor you can award to anyone. *Hey, bro!*

Hi, Dad. Hi, Mom. That's different.

Sam convinces his mom to settle on the sofa for the rest of the night and wait for a phone call—or better yet, for the door to open and her husband to walk in. At last, we hear what we're waiting for: Sam's uneven footsteps coming down the hall.

Marius stands by the dresser, where there's a lamp. He times it perfectly, switching on the light as the door opens so that Sam sees both of us immediately.

"Don't yell," I whisper.

Sam's eyes dart between me and Marius. He steps into the room and shuts the door behind him. "I won't ask how you got in here." He shoots a look of daggers at Marius. "Not after the library."

Marius shrugs. "Sorry."

Sam turns back to me. I'm sitting on his bed with the baby album beside me and his black cat curled in my lap. I hold up the book to show him—and then my arm. Since I didn't plan on being here more than a few seconds, I didn't bother to reverse myself. "I lied to you."

"You *are* J.D." Sam's voice rises.

"I go by Jadie, rhymes with Sadie." His eyes bore into me, and I swallow. "But yeah, I'm J.D." What am I supposed to do? Hug him? Shake his hand? Awkward. Easier to sit here, petting his cat.

But if he calls for his mother, I will hit the button on my bracelet and disappear.

I am absolutely not ready to meet Mrs. Lowell.

Sam looks just as uncertain. He shifts from foot to foot and rubs his hand across his eyes. "You're my sister."

"Technically." I know how dumb that sounds as soon as I've said it.

"What do you mean, *technically?*"

"FYI, we don't have a lot of time for family reunions," Marius says. When Sam glares at him, Marius tries to explain. "I know it must seem like we're aliens, beaming in and out. But the explanation is even weirder. You see—"

Sam interrupts him. "You're traveling through an alternate dimension."

"Oh." Marius sags. "Dang, Jadie, he *is* smart."

"Did you think I wouldn't figure it out? I've known about other dimensions since I was old enough for my dad to explain the basics. You stole my computer with all my multidimensional work. You disappeared into thin air, which is impossible unless you left in a direction I can't see. Not to mention, this happened right after I met a girl with the same birthmark as my sister, except perfectly reversed." He runs a hand through his tight curly hair. "Do you know where my dad is?"

I shake my head. "We were returning the baby pictures. Then we overheard you talking to the cop."

"*You* had the album. I thought my mom . . ." Sam rubs his hands over his face again. "Okay, never mind. Dad is missing, and you came back. This isn't a coincidence. He studies dimensions, and you can move in and out of them."

"It's connected," I assure him. "There are beings in 4-space who've been interfering with people's lives—yours and mine especially. Marius and I talked this over while we were waiting for you, and we've decided to ask our mom and dad for help."

"Dad's *missing*," Sam repeats, as if I'm dense. "And Mom is . . ." Suddenly his face lights up, and for the first time, he smiles. "Mom is going to flip out when she sees you! She never believed you were dead!" He puts his hand on the doorknob.

"No!" The cat leaps off my lap when I stand and point a finger at Sam. "Stop! Not *your* mom and dad." I wave the finger between Marius and myself. "*Our* mom and dad."

"What?"

"Marius and I are adopted. When we tell our parents what's going on—"

"*I cannot allow you do that, Jadie.*"

Even in a whisper, Miss Rose's voice fills the room.

25. SAM

Sam snaps his head left and right, searching for the source of this voice, while Cleo yowls and shoots under the bed. Meanwhile, Sam's long-lost sister and the boy named Marius turn toward each other with panicked expressions. Marius dives for a backpack on the floor, but before he can reach it, both he and Jadie vanish, their bodies contracting to thin lines and disappearing. They must be moving in a direction unperceivable to human eyes. Intellectually, it's fascinating. *Kata and ana are real!*

But when giant fingers swell into existence and swoop toward Sam, intellect flies out the window. He whirls toward the door. Pain stabs through his knee at the sudden movement, and his leg gives way, betraying him.

The disembodied finger segments slither around his torso. "Be still, Sam," says the voice. "I am trying not to hurt you."

Mom! Sam almost shouts, but he stifles his cry, protecting his mother from this thing. The fingers constrict around his chest, lifting him into the air. His bedroom disappears, like it's been squashed into something flat, while his body soars into a space filled with a dim reddish light, unidentifiable shapes, and an acrid, oily smell.

He's not in his own universe anymore. Sam yells wordlessly in protest, pummeling the huge fingers wrapped around his body with his fists. That disembodied voice speaks again, louder than before, but there's something strange about the sound of it, and he misses what is said. He does, however, stop punching his captor. Flying through a terrifying, indescribable world is bad, but it occurs to him that if he frees himself, he'll be in for an even more terrifying fall.

Finally, the way ahead brightens. Sam can't properly make out his surroundings despite the light, although he does see Jadie and Marius. They're lying on their backs with their arms and legs splayed like bugs pinned to a specimen board. A moment later, Sam finds himself in the same position. When he tries to push himself upright, it's as if his body is glued to the ground. His heart pounds while he struggles.

Jadie's hand touches his arm, and she says something that makes no sense at first. Then the words untangle in his head, the way a heavy accent becomes understandable after a brief delay. Something about *intense gravity* and *don't fight it*.

He turns his head to face her. "I can't hear right." His words are mangled too.

"Sound is weird here. You'll get used to it."

She's right. When Jadie starts shouting at the empty space above her, he has no trouble making out her words. Unfortunately, they don't make any sense. "I guess you're not playing around this time!" she hollers. "No pushing me off the Transporter and watching while a meeker tries to eat me? Good! I'm tired of pretending."

A small blue orb appears above them and inflates like a balloon until it's the size of a beach ball. Sam's skin crawls. It's an eyeball with no white around the iris and a horizontal slit for a pupil. "There will be no pretense between us now. I thought you were smart enough to understand my warning, and it seems that you were. You simply chose to ignore it."

"You kept messing with my birth family," Jadie says indignantly. "Did you really think I'd stop trying to learn what was going on?"

In spite of his fear, Sam's heart swells with pride. This girl, his little sister, is fearless. Never mind that they've been plucked out of their universe—Jadie is telling off the creature that took them!

The creature doesn't seem perturbed by Jadie's fury. "I had my hopes. But we are beyond subterfuge. Someone has interfered with my project," it says.

"You mean destroying Sam's program?" Marius calls out. "We're onto you, Miss Rose!"

Sam wonders if his ears have failed him again. His program? Meaning, what—the video game landscape? Impossible! And surely this huge, horrifying creature is not named Miss Rose?

"Foolish children. My project is the development of Sam's program."

"It's a game," Sam states out loud. This makes the least sense. The fourth dimension wants his Escher-inspired game landscape?

"Sam was hit by a car, thanks to you. How have you helped him develop anything?" Jadie challenges.

"Sam was on the track team and would have been the school's star sprinter. There was also a strong probability of a romance with someone on the girls' team. It was unlikely he would receive the software program he needed for this project and even less likely that he would find time to work on it if he did."

"Wait. What?" Sam struggles to lift himself.

"You didn't let him become a track star or get the girl?" Marius sounds outraged. "You monsters!"

"Alia was sent to destroy his computer," Jadie says. "Then Ty. You can't tell me that was supposed to help him. He can't afford to replace it—right, Sam?"

"What?" He's repeating himself, but he's totally lost. Who's Alia? Isn't that the fake name Jadie gave when they met?

"His family cannot afford a new computer," the being from the fourth dimension agrees. "His mother would have contacted his teacher to explain the situation. From that point, there was an eighty-nine-percent probability that the teacher would loan Sam a far superior computer so that he could complete the project faster. But Sam did not report his device broken."

"Because it was stolen by thugs from the fourth dimension," Sam says. "Who'd believe me?"

"Harsh, dude," Marius grumbles. "C'mon, Miss Rose. This gravity sucks. You want to punish us for messing up your gambling? Fine. But don't keep us stuck to the floor like magnets! Take us to a desert or an island and do your worst."

"Marius, shut up!" Jadie hisses. Sam agrees silently. He doesn't want to get stranded in a desert or on an island!

But this creature they call Miss Rose says, "Very well." Long curved talons dive toward them like knives. Jadie shrieks, and Marius yelps like a hurt dog. Sam squirms, trying to get away, as sharp spikes jab his legs and arms and torso.

Something reaches inside his damaged knee. Abandoning any attempt at bravery, Sam howls.

26. JADIE

"**What are you doing to him?**" **I push myself to a kneeling** position. Next to me, Marius makes it onto his hands and knees. But Sam is plastered to the ground, hollering in horror. "Stop it! Leave him alone!" *Torture me, torture Marius, but not poor Sam, who's already been through so much!*

"This cannot be hurting him," Miss Rose says, sounding irritated. Flashes of magenta-colored crystal and flesh-toned blobs hover overhead. "He just dislikes the sensation." The bits of Miss Rose retreat, and Sam sits up, panting heavily.

"Are you okay?" I ask, my chest tight.

"There were *things*! Poking inside me!"

"Put some weight on your leg, Sam," Miss Rose's voice encourages him.

His brow furrows in suspicion, and he glances at me. I nod because I think I know what Miss Rose has done. He gathers his legs beneath him and pushes to a squatting position. "It holds my weight!"

"I cannot repair the ligament that was torn," Miss Rose says. "But I have replaced it with wire on your kata side. It will never break, and it cannot be detected by any device in your world. I have also injected the three of you with a chemical that temporarily enhances your muscles. The effect will wear off as your body consumes it, but for now, you are strong enough to hold yourselves upright. Satisfied, Marius?"

"I guess so," Marius answers grudgingly.

Gravity still pulls on me, so I sink into a comfortable sitting position. If this strength is going to wear off, I need to conserve my energy. The boys copy me, Sam groping at his knee like he's trying to locate the kata-side wire.

"I don't want to sound ungrateful," he says. "If you fixed my knee . . ."

"She's the reason you hurt it to begin with," Marius reminds him.

"I get that," Sam says. "But if she can talk to us on Earth, why do we have to be here? Can't she put us back in my room?"

"No, I cannot," Miss Rose says. "Someone removed your father from your braneworld. Until I figure out who—and where they have taken him—we must speak out of sight of others. You are in my private chamber."

"Wow. Can I get the number of your decorator?" Marius asks sarcastically.

I look too, now that it doesn't hurt my neck to move my head. The glowing light in this place pulses, like it's coming from a fireplace. But the source isn't visible, and in spite of the light there are many dark, unwelcoming corners. *Too many* corners. I stop counting after fifteen. If there's any furniture here, I can't see it.

"But my mom," Sam insists. "You can't do this to her. If I go missing—it'll kill her!"

"Your mother *is* in a fragile state," Miss Rose agrees. "I have every intention of returning you *and* your father, once I have found him. A mental collapse on your mother's part would interfere with my plans. You three wait here. I will take care of Holly Lowell."

"What do you mean?" Sam pushes to his feet. "Leave her alone!"

"I am going to help her, Sam. Inject her as I have done you, except with a chemical that will assure she wakes many hours from now rested in mind and body." That blue eyeball swoops over them again, close enough that Sam ducks. "Stay put. If you wander off, you will not only use up your strength faster, you might get hurt."

"By meekers?" I haven't forgotten that Miss Rose practically confessed to arranging that little scare.

"By meeker *traps*. I dislike vermin in my residence. Think of mousetraps, except you will not see them until they snap closed."

Sam promptly sits down, and I pull my feet close to my body.

The eyeball disappears. There's a squelchy movement of flesh and the scrape of talons on stone—then nothing but the flickering light and the darkness.

"You *know* that creature?" Sam asks.

"For as long as I can remember."

"What the heck is she?"

"Shh," Marius hisses. "She might not really be gone."

"What are those bracelets you're wearing? What did you mean when you said people were sent to destroy my computer? Where have you been since you were kidnapped, and why did you steal that photo album? How did you—"

I hold up my hand. "One question at a time!"

I explain my life as an Agent in a quick recap. The course corrections. The Transporter. The bracelets. How I accidentally discovered myself in his family portrait. "The Seers are supposed to be guiding our world toward peace and prosperity. And we're helping. That's what my parents—my adoptive parents—believe."

"But they're not," Marius interjects. "They're gamblers using us for their own amusement. Our world is Las Vegas to them."

"Who told you that, Marius?" Blobby bits of flesh pop into sight, followed by the blue eyeball.

Sam glares up at it. "Is my mom okay? Or were you here the whole time?"

"Your mother is asleep and healthier than she has been in months. I flushed her body of the chemicals your human doctors have been making her ingest." The eye rolls toward Marius. "I will ask again—*who* told you the Seers were gamblers playing a game with your world?"

"It's true, isn't it?" Marius says.

"No, it is not true. Our actions in your braneworld are the opposite of a game."

"You've got a *purpose* for interfering in my life?" Sam asks. "For kidnapping my father?"

"Your father was not supposed to disappear, Sam, and the fact that he has could be disastrous for us all. If you want to speak in metaphors, your world is not Las Vegas. It is a petri dish in our research laboratory. We are cultivating something we need, and you and your father are supposed to be creating it for us."

27. JADIE

Miss Rose's explanation makes more sense than anything I've heard so far, but Marius sputters indignantly, and Sam exclaims, "A petri dish? Like, you want to make penicillin, and we're the *mold*?"

"I rank you above mold, Sam. Your intellect is essential to our plan."

"What part of your experiment called for me being kidnapped?" I ask. "If you want us to trust you, tell me the truth. Why did I have to become an Agent?"

Miss Rose makes a sound like a sigh. "You were never supposed to be an Agent, Jadie. You were supposed to die."

It's like she slapped me. My head spins; everything swirls and starts to go black. The only reason I don't fall over is because Marius wraps his arm around my shoulders, his warmth soaking into my numbness.

Miss Rose speaks calmly. "Eli Lowell was entering his doctoral program and scheduled to take the wrong courses. He would never have formulated a workable unified theory schooled by the professors he had been assigned. The Seers believed a personal tragedy would delay his education by a year or more, which would put him back on target. The youngest child was chosen to die, because the loss of his wife would prevent him from going back to school at all and his son was integral to our plan."

"Monsters," Marius whispers. "You really are monsters."

"The recent unemployment of Sam's parents was also planned," Miss Rose continues. "It gave him the motivation to work on this program. Additionally, it provided Dr. Lowell with uninterrupted time to work on his mathematical theories. Every event that you perceive as bad for the Lowell family was in fact purposeful for us."

Beside me, Sam moans, his hands on the back of his head. "Mom was right. She said someone was out to get our family. She wasn't paranoid. *She was right.*"

Expressions of outrage lodge in my throat. For years I believed my birth parents threw me away while the Seers thought I was worth saving. Even after I found out the Seers had deceived me—that I was kidnapped, not abandoned—I assumed it was because *they wanted me.*

But they didn't. They tried to kill me so my father would take a different set of college classes. My body shivers violently, and Marius tightens his arm.

"The Seers have no emotional attachment to creatures in the braneworlds. They do not work directly with humans or any other species they study." Miss Rose pauses. "I am the one who arranged for Jadie to be saved. My Agent Becca Martin wanted a child. I gave her one that was otherwise slated to die."

"Why couldn't you hire my dad to do what you wanted?" Sam asks. "You've got these Agents working for you. Why didn't you contact him like you did them and *ask* him to do what you wanted?" His voice rises to a shout. "Maybe that would've worked better than killing off members of his family. Did you ever think of that?"

"We tried it that way with other scientists—*eight times*—and failed. The last time we worked directly with a physicist, his wife became convinced he was conspiring with enemy spies. She reported him to her government, and he was executed before we could intervene. Do you want to know what is really hidden in Area 51 of Roswell, New Mexico? A prototype of the Transporter confiscated by the US government from scientists who were working for us. We get better results acting indirectly through human operatives with no understanding of our true goals but who believe they are saving the world."

"As long as you don't care about killing babies," Sam growls.

"I did not let that baby die," Miss Rose points out. "She is sitting next to you. I am telling you the truth about it now because you need to understand: *I am the only friend you have in 4-space.*"

I lift my head, looking at Sam and Marius in turn. My feelings are mirrored on their faces. The three of us are stuck in a place where we can barely function, at the mercy of a bizarre creature who might be the only thing keeping us alive.

I can't fall apart now. Sucking in a lungful of air, I choose to see past the plan for my own demise. *Breathe, think, and then act. Play smart.* "This thing you need, that the Seers would've killed me for, so Sam and his dad would invent it in the future," I say. "It's a computer program, right? Why do you need a program that lets *us* see in *your* dimension?"

"That is not our goal," Miss Rose replies. "It will not operate in this dimension anyway."

"Why not?"

"The physical laws here are different," Sam cuts in. "Right? The gravity. The way sound travels. Electromagnetism must be different too. I'll bet electricity doesn't work here. I mean, this place is lit by *firelight,* isn't it?"

"Very good, Sam." Miss Rose practically purrs. "The nature of gravity and electromagnetism changes at the transition point between your braneworld and ours. The Transporter is the outer limit of any physical laws you would recognize, and electricity as an energy source does not exist here."

"Then why do you care about the program?" Marius asks.

"Do you remember the *Belvedere* drawing by Escher? What did I teach you about that?"

Marius looks panicked, like he's been called on in class without warning, but I remember the lesson. "You can sketch that building on paper, though you could never build it in three dimensions. But in *4-space* . . ."

"That is correct. The Belvedere could be built here."

"So," Sam says, reasoning it out. "Computers that work in a three-dimensional universe are useless in the fourth because electricity is impossible here. But if physical properties alternate between dimensions—in a *fifth* dimension, electricity should work."

"Fifth dimension?" repeats Marius. "There's a *fifth* dimension?"

Sam leans around me and says to Marius, "My dad says there's at least eleven."

"You are correct. Physical forces such as gravity and electromagnetism behave similarly in alternating dimensions." Miss Rose explains. "Even-numbered dimensions are dismally alike—crushed by gravity with no way to generate energy from electrons—while odd-numbered dimensions are full of potential. We can use human technology in 5-space, except that we are as blind there as you are here. If we could see well enough to construct a Transporter there, it would solve limitations of transportation caused by the gravity here. But my *clianthh* has more ambition than that. We want to *colonize* the fifth dimension, much like humans would like to colonize your moon or the planet Mars. In 5-space, my people could evolve, physiologically and technologically. When this *clianthh* was founded, we gave ourselves the name *Aallhoassha*—which loosely translates to 'Skybound'—with that goal in mind."

"What's a *clithith* . . . ?" Marius imitates the word.

"*Clianthh.* You have no word for such an association. We are not a company, because we are not paid employees. We have a strict hierarchy of labor—Seers, Technicians, and Drones—and we communicate chemically, similar to a hive in your world. But we do not have a communal mind or a queen. The closest concept you have is a *clan,* although members of a *clianthh* are not genetically related. Our *clianthh* acquired your braneworld, along with several others, to research and develop what we cannot create here in 4-space."

I take the Seers' plan to murder me pretty personally, but that last statement demonstrates how little my life or death means to them. Humans are lab specimens under a microscope. The whole thing is almost too horrifying to take in, but I know we're lucky Miss Rose is explaining herself instead of squishing us and starting over with a new batch of mold.

"Marius," Miss Rose asks, "are you ready to tell me who gave you false information about the Seers? Because you must realize by now, whoever it was has taken Dr. Lowell."

Marius looks guiltily at Sam. "Dave and Steve. They call themselves Resisters and said they want to save our world from the Seers. Their real names are something like Daffid and Shteffy. But longer than that."

"*Dhaffyidhre* and *Shteffrynha*?"

"Maybe. You know them?"

Miss Rose's eyeball withdraws. Ripples of her body move back and forth. Her talons click on the stone floor. "No," she says finally. "This is worse than I anticipated. Those words mean *Darkness* and *Storm* in our language. It is the name of a rival *clianthh*. I thought Dr. Lowell had been hidden by another Skybound Technician who wanted to coerce him into finishing the mathematics and claim credit for my project. That would be irksome to me but not dire to your father or our *clianthh*. However, if these individuals are calling themselves Darkness and Storm, we have been infiltrated by something much worse."

"Like what?" I demand. "Who has Sam's dad?"

"Intruders. Spies and thieves. If they cannot steal what they want, they will destroy the experiment to make sure Sky-bound does not have it."

I swallow. "Destroy the experiment. You mean the computer program, Sam's dad, or our world?"

"As many of those as they can get away with."

28. JADIE

Her prediction flattens us more thoroughly than fourth-dimensional gravity. After a horrified moment of silence, Sam exclaims, "You can find them, right? Before they hurt my dad or—"

Destroy the earth. Sam doesn't say it. Is it possible? There's only two of them.

Miss Rose hesitates longer than I like and sounds uncertain when she does answer. "I intend to try. The stakes are high for me personally and disastrous for my *clianthh*. The problem will be identifying these spies when technically they should not exist."

A hand the size of a pony slams down in front of us. My skin crawls at the sight. It has six fingers with far too many joints bending in ways that don't make sense. But what I think Miss Rose wants us to see is the spiky magenta-colored stone embedded in her skin, the same stone I saw hovering above me when I was stranded in 4-space, and the same stone from the ring on Miss Rose's three-dimensional avatar.

"This is a loyalty stone," Miss Rose says. "Since my species cannot use electricity, chemistry is our technology. To join a *clianthh*, an individual submits to chemical branding via a crystalline stone excreted by the Seers."

Marius makes a face and whispers, "Did she say *excreted?*"

"Shh." I hush him.

"Any action deviating from the good of the *clianthh* results in immediate release of chemicals that flood our bodies. Even the thought of such an action or fear of failure triggers punishment from the loyalty stone. It should be impossible to betray one's *clianthh* because the very intention incapacitates the betrayer."

"Then how do you explain Dave and Steve getting into your *clianthh?*" I ask.

"I cannot." She falls disturbingly silent. Her hand and the embedded stone disappear, and the staccato clicking of her talons suggests that she's pacing in agitation. "Unless . . ."

When she doesn't continue, I call out, "Please, Miss Rose. Keep talking. If you're thinking this through, we want to follow along. We need to understand."

"It is only a story I heard when I was a Youngling in the Breeder nests, long before I pledged loyalty to a *clianthh*. A bogeyman tale, you might call it on Earth. Something to frighten Younglings into compliance." She pauses again, then proceeds with what seems like embarrassment. "It was said that aberrant individuals would implant a loyalty stone *inside* their bodies before submitting to a traditional, external branding. The secret stone held a greater sway over their behavior, but warring chemicals made them prone to insanity and violence, creating what humans would call a psychopath. Until now, I thought such a thing was as apocryphal as your Bigfoot, but I do not see any other way for such spies to exist."

I swallow hard. "That's who has m— Sam's father? A couple of psychopaths?"

"Their infiltration of this *clianthh* cannot be recent." Miss Rose doesn't answer my question, but the shifting cross-sections of her body indicates that she is still pacing. "It is unthinkable that spies could arrive and strike immediately at the heart of my project—at a pivotal moment—while attempting to subvert two of my Agents."

And possibly succeeding, in Ty's case. What did he say on the phone to Marius? *She doesn't want me to involve Sam in my plans. So I won't.* He must have gotten the spies to snatch Sam's dad instead, that rat!

Meanwhile, the chemical boost Miss Rose gave us is wearing off. My body feels like I'm wearing a suit of chain mail. Marius is sagging, while Sam has slid down onto his back. Miss Rose continues to pace, her words tumbling over each other like pebbles rolling downhill, becoming a landslide.

"If these intruders have been here for a long time, they may have interfered in prior experiments. They may be the reason our promising scientist Erastus was betrayed and executed before I could save him. His journal went missing after his death. I thought his wretched wife burned it, but if these spies were present then . . . and I missed it . . . I have failed in my duty . . ."

"J.D.," whispers Sam. "She's spiraling."

He's right. Miss Rose sounds like she's on the verge of a panic attack. That stupid crystal in her hand is pushing chemicals through her body to punish her for *thinking* about failure.

"How do we find them *now*, Miss Rose?" I ask loudly, to refocus her. "They must be operating in the vicinity of our universe if they're working with Ty, right? Could they be, um . . ." What term did Miss Rose use earlier? "Rival Technicians?"

"No." That firm response slows the avalanche. She speaks as though careful thought is going into each word choice. "Individuals unbalanced by conflicting loyalty brands cannot function at the level of a Technician. They must be Drones. But that does not narrow the field. Drones outnumber Technicians ten to one. I could detect them in a screening, now that I know what to look for, but if they suspect I have discovered their plot to steal that computer program for another *clianthh,* it will drive them toward their backup plan—which I assume is obliterating our experiment past redemption."

That brings us full circle—back to killing and smashing and planet-destroying.

But Miss Rose's voice grows stronger as logic prevails over panic. "I suppose they *pretended* to be loyal, serving both *clianthhs,* which may have allowed them to survive decades of duplicitous behavior. Now they have taken drastic steps that compromise their loyalty in my *clianthh.* They will be suffering the consequences, and their desperation will only grow. Their hold on sanity will rely on how close they are to achieving their secret goals for Darkness and Storm."

I sink back onto my elbows, my head barely held above the ground. "Does this help you *find* them, Miss Rose?"

"In a way, yes. I have a plan." Miss Rose's voice has returned to a purr, and her blue eyeball reappears as she leans over us. "Unfortunately, it requires using my favorite human as bait."

29. JADIE

I can think of at least a hundred things I'd rather do than sneak into the house of my next-door nemesis in the middle of the night. But here I am.

Marius and Sam watch from below while I climb a tree outside the Rivers family home. "You can step from that branch to the roof of the porch," Marius whispers. "But be careful!"

"Don't fall!" Sam adds helpfully.

Now I have *two* protective brothers. They aren't happy I'm doing this, but it has to be me. Miss Rose said so.

I can't be placed in the house by the Transporter because that would alert Ty and any 4-space spies nearby that I'm working with Miss Rose. How else would I get the coordinates? It has to appear that I'm acting on my own. So I climb the tree.

Miss Rose's plan is complicated, and if that were the only thing I had in my head right now, I'd feel lucky. But there's *everything else*—the real explanation for course corrections, rival clans vying to colonize a fifth dimension, and, oh yeah, my birth family.

It might be selfish, considering the danger we're in, but I

wish Alia were here instead of on spring break with her family. She'd absorb this in a snap. The one time she convinced me to play *Cosmic Knight,* she made me study a chart describing the different types of players, the planets they came from, and their attributes. I thought it was too much stuff to memorize for a game, but climbing the tree outside the Rivers house now, I *wish* I had a chart to keep everything straight.

DIMENSION	ATTRIBUTES	PLAYERS	SPECIAL POWERS
5-space	Reasonable gravity Potential for electricity Normal sound waves (?)	None—yet	_____
4-space	Crushing gravity No electricity Weird sound waves Chemistry as technology	Miss Rose Dave Steve	Size Strength Can see in 4 dimensions Can reach into 3-space and do whatever they want
3-space	Reasonable gravity Electricity Normal sound waves Used as a petri dish by 4-space (!)	Jadie Marius Sam Ty	None, absolutely none

Then again, maybe not. It would be depressing to see how doomed we are when putting one foot in front of the other is the only thing I can do to try to save Sam's dad—and maybe our whole world.

The gap between the tree and the porch roof isn't large. I make the leap, even with a backpack throwing off my balance.

"Third window," Marius whispers.

I wave my hand to shush him. I remember my instructions, and I hope Marius remembers his. Miss Rose won't be able to rescue us if we get into trouble.

"I cannot be nearby," she told us. "If the infiltrators know I am on their trail, they will take Dr. Lowell and run—or kill him outright."

I didn't like the look on Sam's face when Miss Rose said that. My own fear for his dad—I shove that out of my mind. Someday soon, I'll have to deal with my feelings about my birth parents. But for now I'll work better if I keep thinking of them as *Sam's* parents, not mine.

According to Marius, Ty keeps the window of the upstairs bathroom unlocked as a means of secret exit from his house. Or he did until he discovered how to call the Transporter. I hope no one has checked the lock since then.

Squeezing my fingers under the frame of the bathroom window, I give it a tentative shove, and it slides open easily. Ty must keep it slick and silent with WD-40.

I lower the backpack in, slide feetfirst through the opening, then shut the window behind me. If all goes as planned, I won't be leaving this way.

The bathroom looks like the one in my house, except reversed. The door to the hallway is open. Wiping my slick hands on my jeans, I stick my head out.

This isn't the first time I've been in someone's house uninvited. My original visit to the Lowell apartment was one of many course corrections requiring me to trespass. But I've always tackled those missions believing the Seers calculated events so I wouldn't get caught. Plus, there was always the Transporter to extract me if I got into trouble. Never have I entered a house via a window—a house owned by people I know—with no chance of rescue from the fourth dimension.

Swinging the backpack over my shoulder, I creep down the hall. There isn't any light shining underneath Ty's door, but that doesn't mean he's not awake, hunched over his laptop plotting world domination.

Taking a deep breath, I fix my ponytail and hopefully my resolve, then turn the knob with excruciating slowness to ease the door open a couple of inches. When my eyes adjust to the darkness, I make out Ty's computer on his desk, along with the other item I need for this mission. Sam's older, bulkier laptop sits on a dresser next to the bed, where Ty lies burrowed in a balled-up mess of sheets, snoring softly.

Crossing the room and unplugging Ty's laptop takes mere seconds. If I wanted to steal it and escape, I could.

If only the plan were that simple.

In the months since I passed my training as an Agent, I've performed over a hundred missions, most of which consisted of one or two simple steps. Steal this bike and abandon it two blocks away. Take the last seat in this subway car and don't give it up no matter who glares at you. Some Agents receive more complex assignments—like Dr. Rivers performing an emergency tracheotomy with the inner workings of a ballpoint pen. But there's usually only one task to focus on.

For this mission, I have a list of tasks, backup tasks, and a few *if-all-else-fails* tasks. Miss Rose put the plan together and gave it a forty-percent chance of success. That doesn't sound good, but it's the best she could do. She promised to calculate other possibilities once the mission was underway.

Lacking any better ideas, I put Ty's computer into my backpack, making sure that some of it is visible, sticking out the top.

Next comes the part where I have to act like an amateur, which pricks my pride. Telling myself, *Do it for Sam and his dad,* I "accidentally" stumble into the desk chair.

Ty startles awake, thrashing around in his tangled sheets before freeing himself and launching out of bed. Thankfully, he's wearing a T-shirt and running shorts. I was afraid he might be in his underwear—and that's something I *do not* want to see, even to save the world.

"Hello, Jadie," he says, smoothing down his hair. "I was expecting you."

"In your sleep?"

He smirks. "At some point. I suppose Miss Rose sent you? Are you out there, Rose? Listening in?"

"She's not here," I tell him truthfully. "But Marius told me what you're up to, and I don't like it. If this program stays unfinished, the Seers will finally leave the Lowells alone." I shift my position to get closer to a certain glass jar. "Why are you doing this? What did Dave and Steve promise you?"

"Use of the Transporter. And a way to see in 4-space." If it were me who'd been woken up from a sound sleep, I'd be slurring my words and rubbing my eyes. But the evil mastermind is surprisingly alert. His eyes zoom in on my backpack. "You're wasting your time with my laptop. This is where I transferred Sam's program." He picks up a tablet from his bedside table.

Oh boy. *That's* something we didn't anticipate. I hope Marius is hearing this through the open connection on my phone, which is tucked into the front pocket of my backpack.

"All I need are the mathematical algorithms of a unified theory, which your father, *Dr. Lowell,* is working on, and then—" Ty holds the tablet in front of his face and scans the room with it. "We'll be able to see 4-space the way they see it. Or as close as we're going to get. So steal my laptop if you want, but there's no point."

The tablet is a surprise, but it doesn't stop me from implementing the next part of the plan. Scowling at Ty like he's outsmarted me, I remove a laptop from my backpack and plunk it down on the desk.

But not Ty's laptop. Marius's isn't the same model as Ty's, but they look enough alike that Ty probably won't notice from across the room—and any spies watching from 4-space shouldn't know enough about computers to tell the difference. Then I lower the backpack with Ty's computer to the floor and nudge it under the desk with my foot for Marius to pick up later. Bait and switch complete!

Now I need to escalate the hostility in this interaction or Ty won't be fooled by what I do next. "If Dr. Lowell is my father, you should be ashamed about helping your four-dimensional friends kidnap him. How do you think his son and wife are going to feel? They already had one member of their family disappear!"

Ty shrugs one shoulder. "It'll be worth it when they're reunited with their missing daughter. Your father seemed to think so."

I'm not surprised Ty gave away my identity to Dr. Lowell. If everything goes as Miss Rose planned, I'll be meeting him soon anyway. But I pretend to be shocked. "You told him about me? What if I didn't want him to know?"

"C'mon, Jadie. You kept spying on the Lowells. Of course you wanted to meet them."

"What about *my parents*?" I point in the direction of my house.

Ty shrugs again, with both shoulders this time. "Split custody?"

He obviously never gave it a thought, and that ticks me off. I don't have to fake my hostility now. "You jerk!" I close my fingers around the glass jar with the preserved baby shark and hurl it at him, aiming to intercept the footboard of his bed along the way. I'm afraid it won't break if it just hits Ty.

The post on the footboard shears the top off the jar like a glass bottle in a Western bar fight. Preservative fluid drenches Ty and the bed. The baby shark lands on his pillow.

"Ugh!" Ty flings his tablet onto the dresser, out of danger. "What is *wrong* with you?"

He shakes the liquid off his body, and I step back to avoid getting splattered. It's important that only Ty stinks. If I mark myself, the spies could guess what I'm up to. But if it's their own agent affected—and it looks like something that happened in a fit of temper—we're hoping they won't suspect it was planned.

"Ty?" Mrs. Rivers voice calls out from down the hall. "Are you okay?"

Here's the last thing I'm counting on: Ty's parents. "Your mom's awake," I say for Marius's benefit, in case he can't hear Mrs. Rivers over the phone connection. "I'm going to tell her and your dad everything!"

I enjoy the look on Ty's face for about two seconds. Then a fleshy finger appears around his waist at the same time that something grabs me around the middle. Ty disappears, and I'm pulled out of the room—not with the kata movement the Transporter uses, but something different. Entering 4-space feels like a yank, while returning to Earth is more of a drop. That's what's happening now. I'm dropping and dropping and dropping—traveling ana.

"*Can transportation work the other way?*" Alia asked Miss Rose in that lesson months ago. "*Ana out of this world and kata back?*"

Miss Rose suggested we try it with the paper maze, and Ty demonstrated by stabbing his pencil point through the paper.

"*Reversing the ana and kata directions during Transportation is possible, but not advisable. Your universe is delicate.*"

The drop ends with a sucking, clinging resistance before I

break out of my braneworld and hurtle forward into the colors and shapes of 4-space.

I am literally in the hands of a desperate infiltrator. But that's part of the plan. Miss Rose hoped they would be keeping a close eye on Ty and intervene at the hint of any threat to him.

Ty is being carried away with me. That's also what we wanted.

Being ripped the wrong way out of my universe? That wasn't part of the plan.

I have no idea if Miss Rose can follow us this way.

30. SAM

The last thing Sam hears from Jadie over Marius's phone is something about Ty's parents. Then a woman's voice cries out in alarm, followed by a man's voice, thick with anger. They aren't speaking close to the phone, and a roll of thunder drowns out most of their conversation.

"…you think he's hurt?"

"…foul stink…make him pay for the cleaning…"

"Where…"

"…out the bathroom window, like usual."

Marius sucks air through his teeth. "Aw, man, Dr. Rivers knows about the window."

Lightning illuminates the sky, and thunder rumbles again as Marius drags Sam into the shrubbery to hide. Sam braces for the sharp pain that usually accompanies any abrupt movement of his leg, but it doesn't come. Whatever Miss Rose did to his knee worked.

"Did the spies grab Jadie and Ty?" he asks Marius.

"Yes. And she left her phone behind so we can hear what's going on. You gotta admit, our sister is an awesome Agent!"

Our sister. Sam has a sister again, and he shares her with this boy. Somehow, that's even stranger than traveling through the fourth dimension and having his knee fixed by a monstrous being named Miss Rose.

He and Marius eavesdrop on the Rivers house, but thunder makes it difficult, and Ty's parents don't stay in the room with the phone. Instead, Dr. Rivers moves around the house, checking every door and window and locking his son out.

"Dang, he's mean," Marius whispers.

Sam shrugs. He has no sympathy for the kid who helped kidnap his father.

Eventually the light shuts off in Ty's room, and a few seconds later, the parents' room goes dark. Marius turns to Sam. "Now it's time for me to do my part."

Sam swallows a sickening sourness inside his mouth. "Are you sure Jadie's okay?"

Marius looks him right in the eye and states what has to be a lie, because how can he really know? "Yes. She is. I'm off to get Ty's laptop and his tablet. Don't move from this spot." Taking a piece of paper out of his pocket, he punches a button on his bracelet and disappears.

If Sam understands correctly, the paper holds coordinates that'll allow the Transporter—the machine they keep talking about—to put Marius into Ty's room. Jadie wasn't able to use it without rousing the suspicion of the 4-space spies, but if those creatures have taken Jadie and Ty to wherever they're holding Dad, they won't be around to watch Marius.

In theory.

To Sam, this whole plan is risky beyond belief, especially the part that required Jadie getting snatched. Forty percent is not an acceptable chance of success when the lives of his father and sister are at stake. They're at the mercy of four-dimensional creatures who can spy on them from outside their universe and reach inside their bodies. Sam doesn't see any difference between the spies who took his father and the so-called Seers who've been interfering with his family for years. The only one he halfway trusts is Miss Rose, who didn't let Jadie die when she was a baby—and they only have her word for that.

Worst of all, Jadie isn't in Rose's hands now, but in the clutches of dangerous and desperate spies. The plan Miss Rose came up with requires pretending to give them what they want.

Seconds later, Marius reappears with Jadie's backpack. "Got Ty's laptop," he says. "Jadie left it under his desk like she said she would. But I couldn't find his tablet, and your computer is gone, along with my decoy. Dave and Steve must have taken them. The room's a wreck. Ty should be drenched and stinking, like we wanted."

According to Miss Rose, odor molecules have a four-dimensional aspect in 3-space, which is what makes them so powerful at triggering feelings and memories. Humans are affected by this extradimensional quality even though they can't see it—just like Sam can't see the repair Miss Rose made to his knee. To 4-space beings, the odor trail from Ty Rivers will produce a brightly glowing trail of bread crumbs, impossible to miss, easy to follow.

Lightning flashes and rain patters against the ground as Sam follows Marius across the neighboring yard and into a house. It's dark and quiet inside, and a clock on the wall reads 5:30 a.m. Sam can hardly believe this is the same night he and his mother sat up late waiting for news of his father.

"In here." Marius switches on the light in a small room at the back of the house. The walls are lined with bookshelves, and there's a desk covered with books and papers. Marius sweeps them aside to make room for Ty's laptop. "Let's power this up…"

"I'll do it." Sam elbows Marius out of the way, wanting to see this thing that cost him a childhood with his sister—that may cost him his father if Miss Rose's plan doesn't work.

"Ty uploaded photos of his room," Marius explains while the program launches. "Then Dave and Steve took pictures from ana and kata, and when those were uploaded, we could see inside desks and stuff."

"And inside people." Sam recoils at an interior view of Marius.

"Yeah. Ew." Marius holds up a hand to block the sight. "What they said we needed was a way for the program to predict ana and kata, since they wouldn't always be around to take the pictures for us."

"More to the point, they want something that creates images of n+1 space no matter what n is."

"Uhhh...English, please?"

"They want to take it to 5-space and have it work there. This program isn't really for our use, remember? Computers won't work in 4-space."

"So, how far is it from being able to do that?"

"If my dad provides the program with mathematical laws that work universally, it will only take a few changes. The computer won't really know what things look like in the n+1 dimension, but it'll have a good guess." Sam rubs his hands anxiously against his thighs. "Except Ty doesn't have his own computer now, so he won't be able to make the changes. He has mine..."

"Your computer is crappy and slow," Marius says. "I'm more worried about the tablet."

"He can't make programming changes on a tablet." The whole point of switching computers is to delay Ty's delivery of the final product—but how patient will those 4-space creatures be? "Miss Rose is following them, right? She's going to be close behind?"

"Don't worry. Dave and Steve aren't going to hurt Jadie or your dad. They don't have what they want yet, and it can't be created in 4-space. They'll have to bring everybody back to our 3-space world to finish it, and when they do, Ty's going to have the wrong laptop."

"Won't that tip them off?"

A house-rattling crack of thunder draws Sam's attention to the window. The trees are whipping around so furiously, Sam's afraid he'll see the Wicked Witch of the West fly by on her broom next.

Marius glances out the window but doesn't look worried. "Ty won't tell 'em we stole his stuff because it'll make him look stupid. Besides, I left a message for him on my computer. He'll stall for time, which is what Miss Rose needs."

"Okay, so these spies need my dad to do the physics and your friend to put it in the program, but what value is Jadie to them? Isn't she…extra?" Did no one else see that glaring hole in this plan?

"That's a good question, young man, and I've got a few more."

Sam spins around in his seat. Marius flinches and turns slowly, his shoulders hunched.

Two adults stand in the doorway, dressed in bathrobes. One's a tall, fiery-haired white woman who looks like she could snap

Sam in half over her thigh, while the other is a short Black man with a serious case of bedhead that doesn't detract one iota from the keen intelligence and laser-point focus of his eyes.

"Who are you?" the man asks Sam. His gaze shoots over to Marius. "What *spies* are you talking about? And *where is Jadie?*"

31. JADIE

After an alarming journey through the kaleidoscope of 4-space, I'm dumped like a sack of bricks into a white room. Ty lands beside me, reeking and wet. "Thanks a lot," he grumbles. "Do you know how much trouble I'll be in when I get home?"

That's his biggest worry? I'm tempted to smack him hard enough to knock him into the next dimension.

I expect gravity to squash me flat, but I'm able to stand without much difficulty. It's not due to the chemical enhancement Miss Rose gave me . . . she made sure that wore off before letting me start this mission so it wouldn't be detected by our adversaries.

"Centrifugal force," Ty says, guessing at my unspoken question. "We're in a moving container, whirling around like a bucket of water on a rope. It counteracts gravity."

"I *know* what centrifugal force means," I snap at him.

"J.D.?"

I freeze, then turn to face the man who's standing beside a desk on the other side of this strange white room. He's wearing a suit, minus the jacket, which is slung over the back of a chair. I recognize him from the pictures in the baby album, although he's more than a decade older now. His expression at this moment is a mixture of hope and pain and astonishment.

I'm not sure what I'm feeling. It's something I have no words for—and no time to deal with. If this man crosses the room and hugs me, which is what it looks like he wants to do, I'm going to lose it. And I *can't*. I have a mission to complete. "Hold it right there." I raise my hand like a traffic cop. "I know *who* you are, Dr. Lowell, but I don't really *know* you. Don't even *think* about hugging me."

He stops in his tracks. I wasn't trying to hurt his feelings, but he doesn't seem offended—only tearful and happy. "You look so much like your mother."

Oh god, he's going to make me cry.

Luckily, one of the renegade 4-space creatures interrupts.

"Jadie!" A high-pitched voice floods the room. "It was naughty of you to make trouble for Tyler! This is not good." In spite of those negative statements, the creature laughs giddily.

Based on Marius's description, this must be Steve, the high-pitched, giggly one who doesn't use an avatar and might be the less sane of the two. According to Miss Rose, the closer these spies think they are to stealing the technology, the more stable they'll act and the more risk they'll tolerate.

So I plunge ahead with my planned speech. "Are you one of the Resisters? I don't know why you think it's okay to kidnap Dr. Lowell, even to save the world from Seers. I don't see how getting them mad at us will make my family safer."

I hope that conveys my major points as quickly as possible.

1. I believe the story you told Ty and Marius.
2. I'm not on your side yet, but if you promise me the right things, you could win me over.

"No, no, Jadie," Steve says. "We brought Dr. Lowell here to protect him. After he completes his work, the Seers will never threaten his family again."

I plaster a gullible smile on my face. "Really?"

Ty narrows his eyes at me, and I drop the stupid smile.

"Why did you make Tyler stink like this, Jadie?" Steve asks. "It is very *loud* to my sensory organs."

"Tell me about it." Ty keeps grasping the hem of his shirt and dropping it, like he wants to take it off but is embarrassed to go shirtless.

"You promised me like I was a prize instead of a person," I growl at him. "You're lucky I didn't break the jar over your head and make you *eat* the shark." I bunch my fists and step toward Ty aggressively. This isn't the impression I want to give Dr. Lowell of his long-lost daughter. But it's important for Steve to believe that dousing Ty with a pungent liquid was a random act, not a deliberate plan to create a beacon.

Ty backs away like he's afraid I'll really punch him, and Steve laughs wheezily. "Naughty children, making trouble. I was not supposed to take Tyler tonight. Dave will not be happy. You forced me to grab you ana, and now we have to move quickly."

Ty tears his gaze away from my fists. "You moved us ana out of 3-space? Miss Rose said you'd have to punch *through* our braneworld to reach us from the ana side . . ."

Darn it, this is not the time for Ty to start questioning Steve. "Are you sure you can keep us safe from the Seers if Ty and Dr. Lowell complete this program?" I ask.

"Yes, yes, Dave explained this!" Steve says impatiently. "The program must be finished to defeat the Seers."

I turn to Dr. Lowell. "Do you have enough of the math for Ty to finish Sam's program?"

He blinks at me. "Sam . . . ?"

I wave his question away. "Yes, I met Sam. We'll talk about that later. Are you close to having the equations? *I'm sure they're not completely finished,* and it might *take some time* to get them done." I don't dare emphasize my words too much, but I stare at Dr. Lowell unblinkingly and hope he gets my message.

Dr. Lowell pulls off his glasses and cleans them on his shirt. Eventually, he says, "I'm tweaking the formulas that describe the behavior of electrons in successive even-numbered dimensions . . . I'm close. *It will take some time,* but I can teach Tyler how to use the formulas in Sam's program." He shoots me a look out of the corners of his eyes.

I press my lips together in satisfaction. He got it.

"I need my computer and my tablet," Ty pipes up.

"I have them." Steve giggles. "I took them when I took you. You will get started right away."

"Where?" Dr. Lowell asks. "Electronic devices don't work in 4-space."

"They do," Ty corrects him. "Just not in this tesseract."

I was wondering why Ty thought his tablet would work in this universe. Dave and Steve have been lying about more than their intentions. Dr. Lowell shakes his head, clearly knowing better, but Steve doesn't give him a chance to argue. "I will take you somewhere safe. Somewhere the Seers will not find you."

I sigh like I'm relieved by Steve's reassurance, but really it's because everything is going almost as we planned.

We'll have to return to 3-space to complete the programming. Steve won't take us back to Ty's house. He'll go someplace unexpected, like China or South Africa. He might take us to another planet. But no matter where we go in 3-space, Miss Rose will follow, tracking us by the telltale scent molecules clinging to Ty.

Dr. Lowell, who isn't in on Miss Rose's plan, asks the question anyway: "*Where* will you take us to do this programming? I know electronics don't work anywhere in your dimension, not just in this containment unit."

"What?" exclaims Ty.

"Yes," Steve says. "That is why we are meeting Dave in 5-space."

My mouth falls open, and my stomach pitches.

Nobody, not even Miss Rose, considered this possibility.

32. JADIE

While I quietly panic, Ty confronts Steve. "What do you mean, electronics don't work in 4-space? What use is the program if computers don't work here? Did you *lie* to me?"

Maybe I *should* punch Ty to shut him up. Our lives are in danger. Possibly all of 3-space.

But I've underestimated Steve. He sounds bonkers with his creepy giggle, but he has an answer. "Electricity works on the border between 3- and 4-space, where the Transporter exists. That is where you will use the program. Any farther into 4-space and you would be squashed by gravity."

Remembering how Marius's flashlight flared and died on the Transporter, I don't think he's telling the truth. But Ty nods grudgingly, and Dr. Lowell doesn't venture a contrary opinion.

"Now," Steve says, "we move."

I have just enough time to tell Dr. Lowell, "Don't be scared!" Huge fingers clamp around my middle—and Dr. Lowell and Ty too—and the white containment room disappears from sight.

Steve's taking us to 5-space, and I don't think Miss Rose

calculated for this. How are we going to get there? Humans can't move from 3-space into 4-space without help from the Transporter or a four-dimensional creature. So who or what is going to lift Steve into the fifth dimension if, as Miss Rose said, her clan has been unable to build a Transporter there? Will Miss Rose be able to find us?

We have Ty's scent trail, I remind myself. *And if Steve can get to 5-space, Miss Rose can too.*

Steve carries us through a place of darkness pierced occasionally by reddish, flickering light. All I can see are cross-sections of Steve's body: a shoulder with rippling muscles, folds of flesh that might be an ear, and tubular strands of hair.

After what seems like an hour but might be only a few minutes, I sense a change in Steve's movement, like he's pulling against gravity. Little white spots dance before my eyes. When Steve speaks, there's an echo, but his voice is less twisty than usual for 4-space. "This is the beginning of a wormhole that burrows into 5-space. Do you know about wormholes, Dr. Lowell?"

I can't see Dr. Lowell, but I hear him. "Yes. My theory accounts for the possibility of connections between the dimensions. I expected them to emanate from the fifth dimension at their earliest appearance or from the seventh dimension at the latest."

"This question is for the two Agents," Steve says next. "What did Rrhoessha teach you about time in the fourth dimension?"

Ty beats me to an answer. "We were taught that Seers can see forward and backward in time. Now I doubt that's true."

"Oh, it is. The higher the dimension, the crazier time gets. Wait until you see what you get in the wormhole: your past— including every past you could have had." Steve chortles in glee. "Enjoy the trip!"

Before I can figure out what he means, we lurch into the tiny, sparkling lights.

And I lose my mind.

I'm an infant in my crib, hugging my favorite toy. It's a bear. It's an elephant. It's a monkey.

I'm in the front of a grocery cart, cranky and crying. My mother pushes the cart. My father pushes the cart. Sam tries to distract me by waving a toy in my face. It's a rattle. It's a pinwheel.

I'm cold and wet and screaming and nobody is coming to get me.

Darkness. Empty, soul-sucking nothingness. I'm not cold. I'm not anything. I'm just not.

Sensation and thought return in a bright explosion, and a woman holds me tightly, wrapping me in blankets. Comforting me.

The memories come fast and fleeting after that, contradicting and overlapping each other. My mother rocks and sings to me—two different mothers. I play with a brother. Marius. Or Sam. I walk to school on a city street, holding Sam's hand, but I also ride a noisy school bus through a suburban housing development with Marius. I celebrate Christmas with the Martins and with the Lowells.

Alia asks me to watch her bracelet for the afternoon. I say yes. I say no.

I turn my back on Sam's computer and chase the cat. Or I dump a glass of water on his computer and leave without ever seeing the family portrait . . .

When my hands and knees touch a solid surface, Steve releases his grip on me. Even though gravity doesn't pin me down, I flatten myself until my head stops spinning.

Someone nearby gags: Ty, dry-heaving. When he lifts his head and wipes his arm across his mouth, I see a look of dread on his face that's probably matched on mine.

"I understand the alternate memories," I whisper, "but there was a horrible blank spot in the beginning—"

"That's probably the past where you died." Ty stares at me bleakly. "Lucky you. Mine was mostly blank because my father never wanted children. I was a *mistake*."

"J.D." Dr. Lowell holds out an arm. In spite of my no-hugging rule, I wrap both arms around him and bury my face in his shirt. It's probably been a whole day since he shaved, but there's a whiff of aftershave on him. I would've sworn on a stack of Bibles that I didn't remember anything about this man, but the scent triggers an avalanche of feelings. Safety. Warmth. Love.

To my surprise, he puts his other arm around Ty and hugs him too. Ty doesn't hug back, but he tolerates the touch for several seconds before pulling away. I sit up and wipe tears from my face, breathing to regain my focus. I can't cry about aftershave if we're going to get out of this alive.

With a sigh, Dr. Lowell turns in the general direction of Steve. "That was traumatic. If you'd given me two seconds' notice before removing us from that tesseract, I would have brought the journal. This was a useless trip without it."

Steve snickers. "I brought it." A leather-bound journal appears, pinched between claw tips. "And Tyler's equipment." Two laptops and a tablet arrive. A mass of cords and cables rains down on our heads.

I don't want to look overly interested in which computers Steve brought—or in the journal, which Miss Rose asked me to keep an eye out for. So I ask, "You carried all that, plus us? How many hands do you have?"

"When the program is finished," Steve purrs, "you can see for yourself."

I shudder. I don't think our lives will be worth much to them after the program is finished, and I don't want *Steve* to be the last thing I see! Then I chase that thought away. I need to stop acting like we're dead because we didn't end up where Miss Rose thought we would. I'm an Agent. I can figure this out.

Step one: What can I learn about this place? The gravity feels similar to Earth's, maybe a little less strong. Sound waves travel normally. Looking down, I see that I'm kneeling on a platform made of the same metal grating as the ones on the Transporter, although there's no sign of a console or port-lock. A bulbous orange eye and a slitted nostril hang over our heads—Steve. Beyond him, I can't see much. The platform is about the size of the toddler playground where I once met Ty, and the whole thing seems to be floating in a dense white fog lit by sparkling lights. The air here is warmer than it was in 4-space, humid and kind of locker-room-smelling.

One of the sparkling lights zooms toward the tip of my nose. I feel the slightest touch, like a fluttering insect, but it shoots away before I can raise my hand.

While I examine our surroundings, Ty untangles the cables. "Don't know where he thinks I'm gonna plug this in," he mutters, tossing aside a power cord. He hasn't noticed the switch of the computers yet.

That gives me a minute, so I get down on my hands and knees and crawl across the platform. I could stand, as far as gravity is concerned, but the fog is thick enough that I'm afraid of accidentally stepping off the edge.

"J.D.," Dr. Lowell says sharply. "Be careful!"

"I'm always careful." My groping hand finds a place where the platform angles downward. It's not steep, but when I lie flat and peer down the length of it, I see nothing but fog and a scattering of twinkling lights. As I watch, the lights coalesce into a denser cloud and stretch in my direction like the tentacle of an octopus.

"I don't think you should wander off." Dr. Lowell grabs my ankle and gently pulls me back from the edge. I start to protest, but Ty is opening one of the laptops, so I scramble back.

He seems shaken by his experience in the wormhole and doesn't notice anything until he tries to wake up the screen by swiping the touchpad. Nothing. He scowls and, for the first time, really *looks* at the device.

Leaning over to block Steve's view of the computer, I wrap my fingers around his arm and squeeze.

Ty tilts his head back to look at me. I have never gotten this close to him voluntarily, and I shouldn't now, considering how he reeks. His gaze slides back to the laptop that isn't his. He punches the power key, which is the way to wake up Marius's computer. The screen brightens and displays a message in small type.

They're gonna kill you as soon as the program is finished. STALL. —Marius

33. JADIE

"**What is the problem?**" Steve asks, his eyeball dipping toward the screen.

"Nothing." Ty dismisses the message with a swipe of his finger. "It was slow to wake up, but it seems fine now."

I let go of his arm and glance at my father. Dr. Lowell read the message over Ty's shoulder. He nods once and picks up the journal.

"Your electric things work here," Steve says. "You will fix the program now."

"Okay, okay already." Extricating a USB cable from the snarl he was given, Ty connects the tablet to Sam's older computer and starts that one up, since Marius's computer is useless to him. While it whirs and chugs to life, Ty glances sideways at me.

"Do you need my help?" I hope he understands I'm offering to cover our deception, because I sure can't help with the program.

"I'll help him," Dr. Lowell says. "I'll do my part . . ." He looks at me. *You do yours.*

Thank heavens, *he* gets it. I don't realize I'm smiling until I see my reflection in his glasses—and his eyes go wide behind them. It's the first time he's seen me smile since I was a baby.

Nope, nope, nope. Not going there. I look away.

My part in this charade is to provide distraction. So I ask that eyeball and nostril hanging over us, "Who built this platform at the end of the wormhole? People from 4-space?"

"Yes. It was meant to be a Transporter like the one at the border of your braneworld. But there were accidents, and it was never completed." The eyeball swoops closer to Ty. "How long until you are finished?"

"Uhhhh." Ty is more rattled than I've ever seen him. His snake-oil slickness has evaporated. "I don't know."

"You told Dave it only needed Dr. Lowell's equations."

"Yes, but inserting them isn't as easy as it sounds!"

"Half an hour." Dr. Lowell places a steady hand on Ty's shoulder. "Then we'll test to see if adjustments need to be made."

"A Transporter out here would be a big deal, right?" I say to divert Steve's attention. "Traveling in 4-space must be difficult with your gravity."

The eyeball shifts, and the curved shaft of something white and sharp flashes in front of me. A tooth. "Yes, Jadie. That is true."

"And 5-space creatures don't mind you being here, building stuff on their world?"

"There is no significant life on this world."

"What about these?" I raise my hands. Flickering lights gather, tickling my fingertips. Inquisitive. Searching.

A muscular limb flashes through my field of vision, scattering them. "This is not significant life. They are like flying insects on your world. A nuisance."

Ty and Dr. Lowell are also surrounded by fluid groupings of light. Dr. Lowell ignores them, tapping keys on Sam's computer while reading from that leather-bound journal. Ty, however, watches the lights with an intense expression. "I'm not sure they're flying," he mutters. "Or if *they* is the right pronoun."

I nod in agreement. *Ty sees what I see. But Steve doesn't.*

An astonishing idea occurs to me.

Miss Rose's clan has been manipulating human lives for decades to create a computerized method of putting together images in a higher dimension . . . while Ty and I—through repeated exposure to 4-space—*are beginning to do it on our own.*

Isn't that a gear? Ty pointed out the first time we hijacked the Transporter together. *And that looks like a roller chain.*

Computers have to be programmed, but human brains

learn and adapt. Especially kids' brains. Steve doesn't suspect it, and neither does Miss Rose, but maybe the technology they want is already developing inside the minds of their human Agents. Because what Ty and I have noticed—and what Dr. Lowell and Steve seem oblivious to—is that the lights don't move like a swarm of insects.

They move like parts of a single organism.

With his four-dimensional eyes, Steve should be able to see more of this creature than we can, but he isn't used to being out of his natural space. He can't put those "slices of pineapple" together into a whole fruit, and he doesn't realize that we aren't alone on this platform. We're in the company of at least one 5-space being who seems quite curious about us.

At that moment, an angry caterwauling splits the air, and the twinkling lights withdraw in streaming rivulets. An eyeball with a steel-gray iris swells into view. Rubbery lips swing so close, I feel and smell rancid breath. "Treacherous little beast," bellows a deep voice that must be the "Dave" we've been waiting for. "You made a scent beacon for Rrhoessha!"

Oh no. Dave is onto me!

"See here," Dr. Lowell begins indignantly, standing up. Then he ducks.

A claw slashes past him and swipes at Ty, ripping through

his shirt. Ty yelps in surprise and pain and gets hauled off the platform like a fish on a hook. For a couple of seconds, he dangles six feet in the air, caught between fleshy bits and talons and that angry gray eye. Then his shirt tears some more. He falls out of it and lands on the platform.

There's blood on his back where the claw sliced his skin, and when I look up, I see the scrap of fabric that was his shirt disappear into a maw of pointed teeth and pink, glistening flesh.

Dave ate Ty's shirt to eliminate the smell.

My ears pound with the sound of rushing blood. Steve is creepy, but Dave is *terrifying*. Our beacon is gone . . . is there still a trail? Can Miss Rose find us?

"No help is coming," Dave growls as if reading my mind. "You will do what we have brought you here to do!"

"I don't know what you're talking about!" Ty yells, sitting up. "I was already doing what you wanted!"

I exhale, relieved to see he isn't hurt too badly. If Dave had eaten Ty along with his shirt, it would've been my fault.

Dr. Lowell unbuttons his shirt and puts it around Ty, leaving himself in a sleeveless undershirt. Ty winces when the fabric touches his wounded back, but he puts his arms through the sleeves.

On the other side of the platform, muscular limbs scramble back and forth while Steve's high-pitched voice complains in his native language.

"No!" Dave exclaims in English. "I will *not* return to our *clianthh* in disgrace." He thrusts his head between me and Ty, and although I can only see disjointed pieces, I have no trouble imagining what those bulging eyes, slitted nostrils, and cruel teeth look like altogether. "You miserable 3-space creatures will not thwart me now."

A horrible pain lances through me, and I look down in shock, expecting to see Dave's talon embedded in my chest. There's nothing there. Nevertheless, breath leaves my lungs in a rush. My mouth hangs open, my chest throbs, but my lungs won't expand. My sight grows dim and my knees buckle.

As suddenly as it began, the terrible pressure vanishes.

"I can see inside you," Dave hisses. "Every one of you. Finish the program *now*, or I will choose another one of Jadie's organs to squeeze!"

I suck air in and out and in again before the spots clear from my eyes. When I realize Dr. Lowell is holding me up, I force my wobbly legs to do their job, but he doesn't let go.

Ty hunches over Sam's computer with Dr. Lowell's sleeves pushed up, holding the journal in one hand and typing feverishly with the other. Dr. Lowell shouts at Dave. I tune out his words because arguing is pointless. I know what's going to happen next.

First Dave tortures me because I'm not needed. Then he tortures my father because they've already got his work. As soon as Ty gives them what they want, we're all dead.

My eyes search the barren platform and decide upon the most valuable item here. The one thing that is irreplaceable.

Wrenching free from Dr. Lowell, I snatch the journal out of Ty's hand and throw myself over the edge of the platform— down the incline, into white fog and unknown 5-space.

34. JADIE

I tumble in a barely controlled body roll, hugging the journal to my chest. Something heavy hits the incline behind me. Talons scrabble on metal. Tucking my elbows to my sides, I roll faster.

This is the stupidest, riskiest thing I've ever done. *An incline usually leads somewhere* is what I was thinking when I went over the side. But now I remember Steve saying there were "accidents" and this structure was never completed.

No sooner have I recognized the danger than the incline ends, jettisoning me into the fog. My stomach spasms in free fall, and a second later, I belly-flop with a *whomp* onto something firm but yielding, like a gym mat. I can't have fallen more than three feet, but it's enough to jar the journal out of my hand.

No . . . I need that!

I scramble into a crouch and scan my surroundings, well aware of the vibrating incline above me and the pursuer on my heels. The fog is dense, but the dark leather cover of the journal stands out in contrast, a yard ahead. I grab it and take off running across the spongy surface with no destination in mind.

This journal is the only thing that can keep us alive until Miss Rose finds us. *I have no value, except that I'm in possession of the only written record of a working universal theory.* While the journal is missing, Dave won't hurt Dr. Lowell, the only person capable of understanding and re-creating it. Ty is replaceable, but he's the only computer programmer Dave has on hand.

Dave won't kill any of us as long as I have the journal.

Beyond that, there is no plan as I run blindly across an unknown landscape. The stuff beneath my feet—greenish brown and knobbly—might be grass, or a shag carpet. *Maybe I'm running across a 5-space guy's rec room while he hangs out with his gamer buddies double-kata from me!*

The white fog is thicker here, which makes it hard to judge distances. When a forest of tall shadows looms ahead, I can't tell if it's a soccer field away, or a mile. But it's the only cover available.

"Run as fast as you can, Jadie!" Steve's high-pitched voice sings out behind me. "You are a little mouse. And I am a lion."

Mouse. Lion. He's going to pounce on me. I veer to my right. Something huge sails over my head, missing me by a wide margin.

Whoa! Maybe my three-dimensional "player" in this deadly version of *Cosmic Knight* actually does have special powers in 5-space.

1. I'm used to the gravity here. Steve is not.
2. I have experience seeing and acting in a dimension higher than my own. I don't think Steve does.
3. I'm small and fast, and I can hide.

Shadows ahead coalesce into fibrous gray stalks. My brain wants to classify them as plants, but who knows what they are. Patting my way along the outside of one, I gather information about its shape in the dimensions I understand.

When my hand encounters a narrow gap between two of the rough shafts, I squeeze into it. I don't know how visible I'll be from the ana and kata directions, but no matter what, I plan on being hard to reach. *Like a cell phone slipped down between the sofa cushions.*

"Jadieeeee," Steve taunts from someplace close by. The stalks vibrate. "Come out of there, or I will rip off your limbs one by one!"

There's a logical flaw to his plan, but I don't point it out. Instead I holler, "Back off, or I'll rip this journal to pieces!" To demonstrate my superior threat, I tear a page out of the book—a blank one—and shred it as noisily as I can.

"Stop!" Steve wails. The stalks cease vibrating, but something large and sepia-colored moves past the cracks between them. He's trying to reach me.

"I know it's valuable to you." I tuck the journal into the back of my waistband. "Because I don't think your people understand the math."

Steve hisses like an angry teakettle. "You think you are smarter than we are?"

I find another crevice and wriggle into it. "I think your Seers aren't as smart as they pretend to be."

"You know nothing about my world!"

"We know a bit. You come from a rival clan, and you were sent here to steal these equations and the computer technology to use them. If you accomplish your mission"—an idea occurs to me—"*Dave* will be rewarded."

A moment of silence follows. Then Steve corrects me. "*We* will be rewarded."

"You think he's going to share the credit? I mean, he's in charge of the mission."

"He is not in charge! We are equals!" The stalks around me shudder violently.

I burrow in the opposite direction. "You and Dave *were* equals, before you came here. But Miss Rose says you've got two different loyalty stones in your body, and that makes you sick, right? Dave told Ty and Marius it was worse for you than for him."

"*What* did Dave say?"

"That you were getting sloppy, making mistakes. He's right. I doused Ty with something smelly on purpose and you didn't figure it out."

The tip of a talon wiggles in my direction.

"Dave's going to double-cross you. But you and I can work together. He's got Dr. Lowell and Ty. *You and I* have the journal."

The talon retracts.

"What do you want, Steve?" I ask, trying to sound conversational while squeezed between musty-smelling, five-dimensional possible–plant stalks. "What's the reward you're hoping for? A higher rank? Miss Rose told me about them. How do they go? Seer, Technician, Drone, and then something else . . . ?"

"Breeeeeder."

"You were probably a Technician in your old clan, right? But when you came to Miss Rose's clan, you had to take a lower rank. If you go back with this journal and Ty's computer, you can rise to Technician again."

His talons scritch and scratch. "Seeeeer."

Of course. Why go to all this trouble to stay in the same position? "You want to be a Seer. You think they'll do that? With you coming back so sick and Dave claiming he did the work? Steve, *you and I* have the most important thing, the journal. If you can get me back to Miss Rose, I'm sure she'll be grateful." Miss Rose never discussed the possibility of converting one of the spies, but it seems worth a shot.

Steve screams, and the stalks thrash wildly, like they've been assaulted by a hyperactive battering ram.

"Miss Rose will reward you better than Dave will!" I shout.

But I must have crossed the wrong line. A stalk in front of me snaps in two. Thick, pungent liquid oozes from the remaining stump, while the top half disappears, snatched from my sight. Three clawed fingers appear in the newly opened space as Steve digs deeper.

"Leave me alone, or you'll never get what you want!" I scream.

A talon swipes in front of my face. Steve is beyond reason—he'll rip me to pieces whether he gets the journal or not. I grope desperately for an opening, but the stalks grow too close together here. The flaw in my plan to squeeze into a small place becomes clear. I have nowhere to go.

Faces flash before my eyes. Mom and Dad. Marius. Dr. Lowell. Sam. A face from J.D.'s baby album—the birth mother I never got to meet. Why didn't I let Sam introduce us when we had the chance?

Steve slices through more stalks. Squeezing my eyes shut so I won't see the end coming, I press myself against one of the fibrous shafts.

It moves.

I open my eyes. The rigid surface I was leaning against folds away from me, sinking into itself until I'm on the verge of falling into a gap wider than the original stalk. A stream of twinkling lights reaches out of the blackness and touches my face before retreating into the void. Beckoning me.

I hesitate. For all I know, this 5-space thing wants to eat me.

Steve screams in his unintelligible language. Stalks peel away to my left and right. Time has run out.

I step into the starry void, expecting a drop, but my body is buoyed by a feathery-soft touch. Invisible tentacles tickle me with warmth and draw me away from the roaring danger. I feel tenderly cared for and safe—for about three seconds.

The tickling becomes a tingle, and the tingle becomes a burn. I wriggle and thrash, but there's no escape from my bindings. The lights bite like a hundred fire ants and pierce me with a thousand needles. Tiny worms crawl through my body, into my eyes and my fingers and the base of my brain.

I open my mouth to scream, but by then, my body has been
utterly
and entirely
conquered.

35. TY

It happens too fast for Ty to react. One second Dr. Lowell is supporting Jadie after an invisible attack. The next, Jadie pulls away, snatches the journal from Ty's hand, and dives over the side of the platform.

"J.D.!" Dr. Lowell hollers, running after her.

A blow from an unseen hand knocks the physicist off his feet. The platform vibrates and bounces as one of the 4-space creatures launches himself into the fog. Pursuing Jadie.

Ty grinds his teeth over the loss of the journal, although he knows why Jadie took it. She's trying to save their lives. Which is infuriating. Ty doesn't want to be saved by Jadie. This is all her fault!

It isn't her fault; it's yours, says a mocking voice in the back of his mind, a voice disturbingly like his father's. *You swallowed their ridiculous Resister story like a fish gulping down a barbed worm.*

"Shut up, Dad," Ty mutters, staring at Sam's crappy computer and the attached tablet. He has messed up. The throbbing claw mark on his back won't let him forget that, nor the sticky blood that makes Dr. Lowell's shirt adhere to his skin. But what can he do to salvage the situation?

Only one thing. He ducks his head and types furiously.

On the other side of the platform, Dr. Lowell climbs to his feet. "Don't hurt my daughter!" he shouts. "If I'm such a valuable commodity, start treating me that way—or you'll never get what you want out of me!"

Dave's answer is chilling. "You do not understand my mission, Dr. Lowell. If I cannot get what I want *expediently,* I am supposed to destroy it so my enemies do not have it either. I have thirty seconds' worth of patience left for the first option. What have you got for *me?*"

Ty watches them while unplugging the tablet from Sam's computer. Dr. Lowell's face registers shock, his shoulders slumping. He read Marius's warning over Ty's shoulder and probably thought he had leverage over these creatures while the project remained unfinished. Ty knew better. As soon as he saw that message, he knew the three of them were dead meat unless...

Lifting the tablet, Ty peers at the screen, briefly scanning the platform before angling the device toward those persistent lights overhead. Aha! Just as he thought!

Meanwhile, Dave taunts Dr. Lowell. "Nothing?" Pointed teeth drip saliva.

"We have a partially working program," Ty announces, standing up and waving the tablet. "Without the journal, I can't finish it. But if you want a *glimpse* of 5-space, here it is."

The tablet vanishes, ripped from his hands. "It is very small," Dave complains.

"I worked with what I had. Get me better equipment, and I'll make something on your scale."

The hanging eyeball twists and disappears as Dave turns kata or ana. "There are holes and gaps." More complaints, but his tone is less snappish.

"Dr. Lowell can fix that, as long as you don't hurt Jadie." Dr. Lowell gives him a nod of gratitude. Then Ty asks, "It's working, right? You're looking into 5-space?"

Dave's silence is enough of an answer. He seems enthralled.

"Look *up,* then."

The tablet, hanging in midair, swivels upward. Dave makes a startled hissing noise, and the visible parts of his body recoil.

The lights they've been seeing aren't individual creatures. They're part of *one* creature, a life-form with a body that, as near as Ty can tell, exists primarily in the fifth dimension. Shaped like a tentacled jellyfish, it has an undulating sack of skin that is only thick enough in three dimensions to produce those twinkling lights.

And it's *huge.* In Ty's brief glimpse via the tablet, it covered the entire sky.

He grabs Dr. Lowell's arm. "Now! Head for the wormhole!"

But the scientist shakes free. "Not without my daughter!"

Have it your way. Ty sprints for the spot on the platform he mentally marked as the way out upon their arrival. Dr. Lowell's overlarge shirt flaps around him as he runs.

The blow comes from ana or kata with a force that sends Ty flying. He skids across the platform, adding a bitten tongue and numerous contusions to his growing list of injuries. "You, stay put!" Dave snarls. "And *you*—" This is directed at the sky. "Do not touch me!"

"Tyler, are you hurt?" Dr. Lowell calls out.

Stop being nice to me. I was abandoning you! Ty flounders, trying to make his arms and legs obey. Before he can get to his feet or even his knees, Dave shouts something that sounds like alien curses and is answered in the same language by another voice. Not Steve—a smooth and silky familiar voice. "Miss Rose?"

Suddenly there are twice as many body parts undulating on the platform, swelling into muscular limbs, shrinking into fingers and toes and unidentifiable knobs. Then three more figures appear out of the fog—humans this time.

Marius Martin and his parents.

At first Mr. and Mrs. Martin support Marius between them, but after a few steps, Marius—who looks as pale and sweaty as he did after reversing himself—shakes them off with some kind of reassurance. They split apart, the parents sprinting toward Dr. Lowell.

Marius runs to Ty and offers him a hand up.

Ty takes it. "You look awful."

"My alternate past *sucked*," Marius replies.

Nearby, Dave howls and is answered by an angry hissing from Rose. Something ropy swings past and narrowly misses Ty's head—a tail? He and Marius step backward, which unfortunately puts Dave and Rose between them and the wormhole.

Meanwhile, a hasty introduction is taking place between Jadie's three parents. The inevitable question gets asked, and Dr. Lowell points over the side of the platform. With a grim expression, Mr. Martin uncoils a rope from his belt, while his wife directs Dr. Lowell's attention to Ty and Marius. "My son will guide you and Ty back through the wormhole."

"I'm not leaving without my daughter," Dr. Lowell protests.

"She's our daughter too. Trust us."

"C'mon!" Marius shouts, gesturing wildly at Dr. Lowell. "We need to get out of here before we get stepped on!"

They do indeed. Ty only got a brief glimpse of Dave on the tablet, but he's not likely to forget it. The barrel-shaped body. Six muscular limbs, each with two appendages serving as hands or feet. An angular face with three eyes. And most horrifying— dual protruding jaws, each with a mouthful of sharp teeth.

Now there are *two* of these elephant-sized monsters on the platform, locked in physical combat. Both Rose and Dave are screaming and flailing wildly in gravity weaker than they're used to. They could roll over and squash a human at any time. Everyone needs to escape by the wormhole—or follow Jadie off the platform.

But the adults are arguing. Dr. Lowell points at Mr. Martin, who's trying to thread the rope through the platform grid. "You can't make a knot with 3-D rope tied to a 4-D structure in 5-space!"

Mr. Martin looks up. "He's right, Becca. There's more to this platform than I can see."

"Then I'll be your anchor." Mrs. Martin takes the rope from her husband and starts tying it around her own waist. "Go with the boys, Dr. Lowell."

"You don't understand how this dimension works," the scientist protests. "Three-dimensional knots won't hold here!"

It's insane to keep arguing. Jadie's lost, and that's too bad, but none of the humans are physically equipped to find her. Ty scans the platform, trying to piece together the disjointed images of the fighting 4-space rivals. To reach the wormhole, they'll have to dodge both Dave and Rose. It would really help if they could *see* properly.

As if summoned by his wish, Ty's tablet appears in midair and plummets toward the platform. Dave howls in anguish at the loss.

Running toward gargantuan creatures he can barely see is not the smartest thing Ty Rivers has ever done, but he throws what little athletic skill he has into it, stretching out both arms to catch the tablet like it's a football. He gets right underneath it, tracking its fall, and the tablet is within his grasp when his body abruptly drops—the metal platform curling away beneath his feet and into the fog.

36. TY

The strange thing about Ty's fall is that it doesn't feel like falling so much as having his shirt pulled inside out over his head. When the platform stops moving, what was once a flat surface curves in an upside-down parabola, the metal snapped in places like toothpicks. Ty finds himself standing beside Marius, who a moment ago was several feet behind him.

"What happened?" Marius gapes at the devastation.

Ty can think of one explanation. "We've been turned around in 5-space."

"You mean reversed?"

Not reversed. Marius isn't puking. Ty doesn't have a migraine. Plus, this platform suffered a lot worse than being flipped over. Mr. Martin, who'd been lowering himself down the side, is now hanging from the grid *above* them. A rope anchors him to his wife, but Mrs. Martin holds the loop with astonishment because her knot has untied itself.

Though the platform is all but destroyed, the people on it are untouched. That suggests *intelligent* agency.

Howls and shrieks turn Ty's attention to the fact that Dave and Rose are still locked in combat. "Where's the wormhole?"

Marius yells above the noise. "I'm supposed to rescue you, but the wormhole's not where it used to be!"

"I don't need rescuing. I'm not a damsel in distress!" But Marius's concern is valid. Ty has no idea where the wormhole is now. His reference points are unrecognizable.

Where did the tablet go? Crushed beneath Dave and Rose? Or fallen through the broken platform into oblivion? He doesn't see Sam's computer with its oh-so-valuable program either.

Ty wants to tip his head back like a dog and howl in frustration. This did not go as planned!

Marius grabs his arm and points overhead. "What's that?"

A cloud of light streams through the twisted hole of the inside-out platform, spiraling around the humans and Rose and Dave. This 5-space creature is probably responsible for the damage done to the platform. What its intentions are, Ty has no idea.

Dr. Lowell shouts, "J.D.!"

Through the broken shaft of the platform, the creature lowers Jadie's limp body. Ty sees no sign of injuries, but she doesn't react to her parents shouting her name. She looks unconscious—or worse—until she descends to within a few feet of the platform. Then her eyes jerk open.

"Cease hostilities!"

Cease hostilities? That's Jadie's voice for sure, but Ty doesn't think she's the one using it.

Rose and Dave pay no attention to Jadie's order. Their flailing and pounding continue.

Lights plunge toward the struggling creatures. Seconds later, their bodies hurtle in opposite directions. Ty and Marius scramble out of the way as something large with tubular whiskers skids toward them.

Dr. Lowell stumbles backward too but doesn't take his eyes off Jadie. "Please don't hurt my daughter!"

"Let her go!" Marius picks up a broken metal shaft like he's going to launch into hand-to-hand combat to save his sister.

"SHE needs Jadie-being to communicate," Jadie's voice states woodenly. "SHE has no other means to communicate with invading life."

Everyone falls silent in the wake of this strange statement. Rose recovers first, her voice emanating from the creature with the whiskers near Ty. "We are not invaders. We are explorers who discovered your world. We did not know there was intelligent life on this planet."

"*World* and *planet* are unknown." The starry web suspending Jadie quivers. "Jadie-being pictures a rock for *planet*. SHE is not a rock. I am SHE. You are with SHE. SHE is here."

"What does that mean?" Marius mutters.

Ty looks around and wishes he had that tablet again. He sees starry tentacles holding Jadie aloft and others surrounding the group, not to mention the spongy, knobbly surface beneath the broken Transporter platform. "I don't think this is a planet," he says as the revelation trickles into his mind. "This whole place is a living being, and the 4-space people tried to build on it."

"Yes," the creature agrees. "Like lice. Jadie-being pictures lice as small beings that live on greater beings."

Whoa. Rose's people traveled through the wormhole to what they thought was a planet in 5-space and started constructing a Transporter on this creature's . . . what? Scalp? Elbow? Armpit? A five-dimensional body part there's no name for? "No wonder there were *accidents*," Ty says.

"SHE did not know lice were alive," the creature intones in Jadie's voice. "*Alive* and then *deceased*. SHE understands knowing and being, but not other alive things that think and be—and cease to be."

"Is there a HE?" Marius wonders. "Or any other SHEs?"

"There is only SHE."

Mrs. Martin puts a hand over her mouth. "How lonely!"

"Please release Jadie!" her husband calls out.

"What you're doing could be hurting her," Dr. Lowell adds.

"Neurological pathways are unharmed," SHE declares. "Jadie-being is not distressed."

Jadie gives them two thumbs up.

Ty assumes this creature can fake Jadie's gestures, if fooling them is her purpose. But why would SHE, if SHE can reach directly inside their minds? The thumbs-up is probably a signal from the real Jadie—which means she's conscious. SHE's not only pulling words and images out of Jadie's head. They're actively communicating.

Something wriggles in Ty's own mind. Not an alien being. Just plain old envy.

"Lice came," SHE says. "Lice died. SHE regrets that SHE did not understand life could become deceased."

"Yes," Rose agrees. "Members of my clan died building this platform. We thought they were accidental deaths. But we are *not* lice!"

"Lice are best made deceased. SHE is curious about life that knows things outside of SHE. SHE reaches through hole where lice appear, trying to learn, but cannot function in flat space. It is regrettable that lice must be deceased when they are so *interesting*."

Ty's heart lurches as the words start to make sense. SHE is apologizing for the need to exterminate the beings who crawled out of the wormhole and onto her body. Because no matter how interesting, lice are unwanted, and she got that idea from Jadie. "Not lice!" he shouts. "Jadie doesn't mean lice! Lice are parasites. We're more like, um...bees. *Think bees and flowers, Jadie!*"

"Good save, Ty," Mr. Martin says with a gulp.

SHE is slow to respond, and the group gazes at each other uneasily. Five, six seconds crawl by before SHE says, "Ty-jerk is correct. SHE is a flower. A *flower* is delicate and beautiful. That is the same as SHE. Miss Rose-teacher is a bee with a hive. *Bees* are useful and productive."

Ty-jerk? When he just saved her parents and her brother from getting squished? *Thanks for that.* Ty simmers, realizing how much influence Jadie has over this being.

Why is it always Jadie who comes out on top?

"My people have a hive too," Dave growls. "We want to come to 5-space."

There's another long pause, as if SHE is consulting with Jadie, and—as Ty predicts—Jadie's opinion prevails. "Darkness and Storm are not helpful. SHE does not like absence of light and atmospheric disturbance. SHE does not want them here."

Dave snarls, his muscles rippling.

Ty's brain jumps immediately to the only action Dave can take. "Dr. Lowell, look out!"

Teeth flash—more teeth than should be possible for one creature to have. Dr. Lowell recoils and trips on the broken platform. Rose lurches to her feet, but sluggishly, leaving a pool of black ichor in her wake.

Twinkling lights sweep over Dave. A horrible ripping sound follows, ending Dave's snarl abruptly. When the lights withdraw, piles of red blobs appear. A pool of sticky goo trickles through the metal grating.

"*That* was not intended," says SHE, sounding startled. "It is regrettable that lesser beings cannot move in that direction."

Ty swallows a mouthful of bile and looks away from the bits of Dave that should be on the inside and are now *regrettably* on the outside. The fifth set of spatial dimensions is apparently detrimental to beings and objects that can't be turned inside out.

"It was unavoidable," Rose says, though she sounds shaken. "Thank you for saving Dr. Lowell. There is another person here, every bit as violent and dangerous..."

"Steve-beast is confined in another part of SHE. He can be made deceased, but Jadie-being says *no* because it is only a bad stone that makes him so un-nice."

"Yes," Rose agrees. "If you can remove the loyalty stone inside his body without killing him, my clan will try to rehabilitate him."

Ty has no idea what a loyalty stone is or what it has to do with Steve being the way he is. But apparently, *Jadie* does. Jadie knows everything.

"The bad stone is out," the 5-space creature announces mere seconds later. "SHE is delivering him to the flat space you came from."

SHE thinks 4-space is *flat*? Ty tries to imagine how vast SHE must be, how many appendages and sensory organs she might have. Could SHE have multiple brains in different parts, like leeches do? And is there, somewhere, a planet SHE lives on, with a universe beyond it? Or is the entirety of 5-space comprised of SHE?

"Thank you," Rose says. "Your mercy is generous."

"The bees are welcome to return to the flower," SHE says. "And SHE will keep Jadie-being to communicate."

Of course SHE will.

All three Martins holler, "You can't!" practically in unison, while Dr. Lowell starts pleading, "Please . . ."

Rose speaks over them. "We ask you to let Jadie go. She is a child. In the world of three-dimensional humans, children are precious. Jadie's parents want to take her home."

"SHE needs Jadie-being." SHE pulls Jadie's body closer to the mass of starry lights, like a toddler hanging on to a toy that adults want to take away.

"I will give you one of my Drones as a replacement," Rose promises.

"SHE does not want them. SHE likes Jadie-being."

"Take me!" Ty shouts. Stepping forward under the shimmering lights and the girl hanging midair, he raises his arms to the creature. "Let her go, and take me. I'm similar to Jadie. You can adapt to me. I *want* to stay!"

Control of the Transporter is lost to him. The tablet and the computer program will end up with Rose, assuming they weren't both destroyed. This is the only thing left for Ty to grasp for himself. And *this*—an ambassadorship to a suggestible, child-like creature large enough to be mistaken for a planet—would be much more than a consolation prize!

Hands grab him from several directions, yanking him away from SHE. They talk over each other, their words a jumble of protests.

Mrs. Martin: "Ty, you don't have to give yourself up for Jadie!" (As if.)

Marius: "Are you nuts?"

But Dr. Lowell speaks the loudest. "It would be an unkind thing for SHE to take *any* of our children—even an unhappy one!"

Ty snaps back, "I'm not unhappy. I'm ambitious!" His eyes fix on the creature and on Jadie's body, which slowly descends toward the platform. SHE has made up her mind, and she has chosen...

"I accept Miss Rose-teacher's offer of a Drone and return Jadie-being so that she can participate in the great battle looming on her world," the 5-space creature says mournfully. "Jadie-being is needed for victory, or sadness will befall her people."

Rejection cuts through Ty like a sharp knife, painless in the first second and agonizing thereafter. The people who clutched at him when he offered himself to SHE let go, their attention turning to Jadie.

"Great battle?" Mr. Martin repeats worriedly.

Jadie's feet touch the warped platform. When SHE releases her, Jadie blinks and clears her throat. "All I said was, I had a soccer tournament to get back for. You know they can't win without me."

While Mr. Martin grabs his daughter in a bear hug, Ty backs away.

SHE didn't consider him, didn't even answer his offer.

He's come out of this with nothing.

37. JADIE

I barely have time to adjust to seeing through my own eyes again before Dad grabs me in a tight hug. Mom slips her arms around me too, although I don't know how she fits them in. It's almost multidimensional.

"I'm sure in your mind, the soccer tournament equates to world domination." Dad squeezes me hard. Mom kisses me twice after Dad lets go, and then I'm awkwardly facing my third parent.

I pull the physics journal from the back of my jeans. "Saved this for you."

Dr. Lowell ignores the journal and crushes me in a hug. It feels good, even though he's breaking my rule.

"I am happy for your reunion," Miss Rose says, "but I want to get you back to 4-space before SHE changes her mind. As it is, I will have to track Ty's scent to the wormhole. I have lost my own sense of where we are."

"Glad my stench can be of help," Ty says snarkily.

I glance at Ty. He's probably furious SHE didn't accept his offer, but his feelings are not my concern. "You don't have to track your way, Miss Rose," I say. "SHE will transport us. I just need to signal we're ready." It was the last idea SHE and I exchanged before she let me go—that SHE would carry us all back to 4-space.

"Let's go," says Dr. Lowell. "My wife must be frantic with worry."

Marius sucks in a shuddering breath. "Do we have to see the alternate pasts again?"

"Not you." Miss Rose's claw tip touches Marius, and he slides to the ground in a boneless heap. Mom and Dad cry out in alarm, but Miss Rose says, "It is better for him to sleep through the trip. The rest of you can handle it."

Dad kneels beside Marius and props up his unconscious body. "Thank you for sparing him."

I'm not looking forward to repeating my own experience in the wormhole, though when I realize what Marius must have endured, I know I got off easy.

Raising my arms over my head, I wave, and featherlight tentacles wind around my waist more gently than Steve's muscular fingers ever did. I brace myself for the connection, but this time SHE keeps her appendages out of my nervous system.

We plunge into the wormhole without warning. There's a

whoosh inside my head, and the insanity of the ever-changing past fragments my memory into a hundred different possibilities. This time, the oblivion that overcomes me in the past where I didn't survive the carjacking is less soul-wracking. Maybe my recent connection to SHE lessens its impact. SHE had no concept of death until SHE learned it from me. Some of that must have rubbed off, because I ride through my nonexistence with relative serenity, knowing it's not reality.

I did live; I am alive, and nothing I see in this wormhole can change that.

SHE will miss Jadie-being. The barest hint of that thought touches my mind as the feathery tentacles release me.

My family was horrified when SHE wanted to keep me, but I never believed SHE would. Not against my will. SHE only needed to understand why I wanted to leave. *I'll starve!* was my first explanation. *I want my family!* was my second. *I have a soccer tournament on Saturday!* was an irrational thought, yet the one SHE fixated on. Nutrition and family are meaningless to SHE, but having grasped the concept of individual lives, SHE finds it fascinating that they could be in conflict.

The wormhole ends abruptly in 4-space—big and dark and crushed by gravity, but somehow *smaller* than where we were. I land on my hands and knees, fight the pull of gravity for one second, then give up and lie on the ground. We're out of danger. I deserve a rest.

Dr. Lowell thinks otherwise. "You are taking us home now, aren't you?" he asks. "I need to get back—"

"I know you are anxious to return to your family," Miss Rose replies, "but there will be a small delay. I retrieved the computers, but I need the journal now."

A trickle of alarm runs down my back. *Are* we out of danger? When Miss Rose has her talons on the theory completed by Dr. Lowell and the computer program created by Sam and Ty, what use is this particular batch of humans? Humans who know the real reason Agents exist and the true motives of the Seers.

Ty seems to be thinking along the same lines. "The program isn't finished," he says quickly. "I only faked it enough to distract Dave."

"I will inspect what you have accomplished," Miss Rose insists.

The journal is in my hand. Remembering that sideways motion is easier than fighting gravity, I slide my body until I'm lying on top of the leather-bound treasure.

The effort is wasted. Large fingers flick me onto my back like I'm a beetle and pluck the journal away.

Ty keeps arguing. "That tablet is too small for your eyes. We need to come up with something more to your scale . . ."

"Tyler, if I wanted to dispose of you, I would have let Dave trample you in 5-space."

Long seconds of awkward silence pass.

Then Miss Rose adds, "I *reward* individuals who do a good job, not punish them."

"Doesn't seem like that from my vantage point," Dr. Lowell grumbles. "You arranged for my daughter to be kidnapped and my son to be hit by a car."

"You're the reason Eli lost his research grant and Holly can't find a job," Dad says.

"How do you know about that?" Dr. Lowell asks.

"We met Sam and took him home to Holly," Mom says. "Before we came to rescue you."

"You are correct on all points except one," Miss Rose replies. "*I* did not plan those changes to Dr. Lowell's life. The Seers did. Things are about to change. When this project is completed, my status will rise. I will be in a position to reward those who helped me. But I must ask Darrien and Becca Martin: Do you plan to tell your fellow Agents what you have learned?"

"You expect us to keep playing along?" Dad asks incredulously. "Pretend we're not test subjects in a giant experiment?"

"My dad'll quit," Ty states. "He thinks he's so important. If he knew he was a lab rat, he'd flip out."

"Your world benefits from this experiment," Miss Rose says. "Terrorist plots have been averted. Unbeknownst to you, a meteor was turned aside from your planet. This experiment is *protected*. If Agents cease to cooperate, the Seers will order Technicians to train new ones, *or*—since you have already created a template for what we want and there are other braneworlds where the product can be developed—they might relinquish responsibility for yours. Your braneworld could end up in the hands of a clan like Darkness and Storm."

"You see our universe as expendable?" Dr. Lowell exclaims. "Our lives of no value?"

One of Miss Rose's huge eyeballs hovers closer. *"I do not. But I am not a Seer. Yet."*

I get it. "If your project is a success, you get promoted."

"I will reward you for your efforts and protect your world."

"How do I know," Mom demands, "that when I get a course correction, it's not going to result in someone else's child being kidnapped?" She addresses Dr. Lowell. "I hope you believe we didn't know. We were told Jadie had been abandoned by her parents!"

"I believe you," Dr. Lowell says. "And I owe you thanks for raising my daughter so lovingly."

"What about Marius's family?" Mom looks at my brother, blissfully asleep.

"He would have died without our intervention. But the Seers envisioned great things from Marius, and so he was saved. You have no reason to believe me," Miss Rose admits, "except for what he saw in the wormhole. This is the only version of his life in which he survived."

A shudder runs through me. I experienced a past where I died. And Ty said his father didn't want children, so I guess Ty experienced multiple pasts where he didn't exist. Or, rather, he *didn't* experience them. But neither of us burned to death in every possible past but one.

"We have to do what she asks," Dad says suddenly. "To keep the children safe. To keep everyone safe."

"I agree," Dr. Lowell replies. "If creatures like Dave and Steve had control of our world . . ."

"Where *is* Steve?" I ask. SHE was able to remove his old clan stone—slipping it out of his body through a 5-space dimension and leaving the rest of him relatively intact. SHE returned him through the wormhole while SHE was communicating with my parents and Miss Rose on the platform. But that should mean that Steve is *here* somewhere.

"He is nearby," Miss Rose confirms. "Can you not smell him?"

"That's me you're smelling," Ty grumbles.

"You need to get over that." I roll my head to look at him. "Miss Rose told me to do it, and it probably saved our lives."

"I smell something like burnt rubber," Mom says. "With cinnamon, if that makes sense."

"He is excreting pheromones that indicate extreme distress," Miss Rose explains. "He is calling for help, like you might dial 911."

"Why aren't you helping him?" I'm not sure why I'm so worried about Steve. Maybe I feel sorry for him. Maybe it's guilt over Dave getting turned inside out. When I saw him leap toward my father—uh, Dr. Lowell—I pleaded for SHE to *Stop him!* I didn't realize what might happen when SHE knocked him aside. Whatever the reason, since SHE—well, actually WE—made the attempt to save Steve, I don't want him to die of neglect now.

"It is not my job," Miss Rose says. "Drones will deal with him. Darrien Martin, do I have your word that we can come to an arrangement?"

"For the sake of the children," Dad repeats, "yes."

"Then it is time you went home. Drones! Take them back!"

Fingers and claws appear out of the gloom, bodies shift, and people disappear one by one from the dark chamber.

Except me.

I'm spread-eagled on the ground, pinned by gravity, while Miss Rose's blue eye with the horizontal slit glares down at me.

38. JADIE

I swallow uncomfortably. "You forgot me."

"I will take you home myself. But not yet."

Not yet? I can't hold back a groan.

"I want to show you something," Miss Rose says.

"I can't see very well here," I remind her.

"I will remedy that. First, let me give you a boost in strength."

I feel the same prick in my legs and arms and torso as last time. Seconds later I'm able to sit up, and I don't feel tired and hungry anymore. But I want to go home more than I want to look at the crystalline rock hovering in front of my face. "Is that gem what you want me to see?"

"It is what you are going to see *with*. This is a four-dimensional crystal. Look through it and you will see reflections from all directions, including the ones you cannot perceive on your own. It will not be like seeing through the eyes of SHE, and it will not put the images together like Sam's program, but from what I have observed, you are starting to do that on your own."

I take the crystal into my hands. It's heavier than it looks, even accounting for the force of gravity, and I assume that's because it has ana and kata extensions. Its many facets reflect dozens of images. "You had this the whole time? Then why did you need—"

"It is four-dimensional, Jadie. It will not help us in 5-space. Humans find it useful, however."

I tilt the crystal back and forth, getting glimpses of Miss Rose. I already saw the real Miss Rose through the eyes of SHE, so the reflected images in the crystal are like a jigsaw puzzle of eyes and mouths, teeth and weird Medusa hair.

"The last human I allowed to use a viewing crystal was the man who started the unified theory finished by Dr. Lowell. So, Jadie, what do I look like to you?"

"Uhhh . . ." I let the crystal thunk on the ground. How am I supposed to answer that? "Powerful."

"Not beautiful?"

"Well, different species, different standard . . ."

"Hold on to the crystal. I am going to show you what beauty looks like in my world."

I clutch the crystal to my chest and brace myself for Miss Rose's fingers, which clamp around my torso. She carries me quite a distance through sparsely lit tunnels before the way ahead begins to glow. We enter a large cavern illuminated with torches and some sort of phosphorescent growth on the walls.

"Look down." Miss Rose helps me adjust the viewing stone.

The kaleidoscope of images shifts to a dozen bloated bodies lying on the floor of the cavern. The pale, flabby creatures remind me of slugs, or maybe giant larvae. Their limbs—six for each—hang from their bodies, withered and useless. An army of 4-space creatures similar to Miss Rose crawls over their bodies. "What are they?" I ask, grimacing.

"They are the Seers." Miss Rose sighs longingly.

"Those . . ." I stop myself from saying *slugs*. "What are the other ones doing, crawling over them?"

"Those are Drones. They feed the Seers, clean their waste, deliver and receive messages."

I have to look away. I. Can't. Even.

Miss Rose speaks with admiration. "Some of the Seers have not moved in centuries. Their minds are in a chemically induced state of hyperintelligence."

"You mean they're on drugs?"

"That does not mean the same as it does with humans. The Seers have advanced to the peak of our species. They calculate the probable future of millions of lower-dimensional beings. They coordinate course directions on your planet and other planets in your braneworld, as well as planets in several other braneworlds."

"*This* is what you want to be?"

"Different species, different standard," Miss Rose reminds me. "One of the Seers below envisioned a spectacular future for a human child who was going to die in a fire. Marius owes his life to that Seer, although it remains to be seen if he will reach his potential. Another Seer decided that your death would set Eli Lowell on his correct course. None of the Seers saw your value."

Harsh. But I think I get her point. "*You* did, though?"

"Yes. I wanted to reward my faithful Agent Becca Martin with a child, but I also saw potential in *you*. Twelve years later, you are instrumental in meeting our goal. Do you know what this means?"

Fame? Fortune? Glory? "No. What does it mean?"

Miss Rose releases a long sigh of satisfaction. "I have foresight, even as an unenhanced Technician. I may become one of the greatest Seers our species has ever known."

Please, Miss Rose, don't become a huge helpless slug that needs drones to clean its poop.

I don't say that. My opinions are unimportant in the fourth dimension. Maybe completely wrong. "You'll make a brilliant

Seer, Miss Rose. But I hope you'll do a better job of standing up to the rest of them on our behalf."

One of her eyes pivots in my direction. "What do you mean?"

It's daring to get this critical, but she brought me here to confide in me, so I plunge on. "My father shouldn't have had to lose his daughter to become a brilliant physicist. It was cruel."

"If I had not arranged for you to be kidnapped, you would not have the Martins and Marius in your life. Would you rather that be the case?"

My head swims with the tangled memories from the wormhole—every past I could have had. It's not fair to ask me to choose between them. "I think you can do better."

"I certainly intend to try." She makes a low noise like a laugh, although I don't see how it's a laughing matter.

"You can have this back." I hold up the viewing crystal. I've seen enough of Miss Rose's hive, her Seers, and her future.

"Keep it," she says. "It is a gift. You will not want to miss seeing your braneworld through it when I take you home."

39. JADIE

An ocean. That's what it looks like. An ocean of stars and darkness and swirling nebula clouds. It seems to go on forever in every direction, but that's true of real oceans too. When you're in the middle of them, it's hard to imagine they'll end.

My universe is vast, but just a membrane in 4-space—and it's covered in Drones. Their job, according to Miss Rose, is to observe and report back to the Seers. For the first time, I understand why Miss Rose was worried about identifying the infiltrators from Darkness and Storm. There are *thousands* of Drones here.

I also remember what Ty told me when we were using the Transporter without permission. *Nobody's watching.* He was wrong.

Miss Rose takes what she calls the scenic route home, passing planets covered by scaffolding. These are other Transporters, she explains, moving Agents to their destinations on other worlds. Nonhuman Agents. Aliens on planets across the Milky Way Galaxy and beyond. I should be stunned by this proof of other intelligent life in my universe, but it feels anticlimactic after meeting SHE.

"Ty said our bracelets are attached to the Transporter by fishing wire. You reel us in and out. Is that true?" I ask.

Miss Rose chuckles. "It is more complicated than that, but he is surprisingly accurate on the basic principle."

Earth, when I finally see it, is covered by more Drones than anywhere else. "They are repairing the damage done when Steve took you the wrong way out of your braneworld. We are not supposed to push all the way through a membrane."

"What kind of damage?"

"Luckily for you, the effect is minimal where the tear begins—at the Rivers house. Your neighborhood suffered a severe storm. People on the opposite side of your planet were not as fortunate. Typhoons. Earthquakes. Drones took immediate action to reduce the impact on human lives, but on the other side of your galaxy, an entire star system was destroyed. Correcting these events will take years, perhaps centuries."

An entire star system? Were there living beings in that system? Were there casualties on Earth? I open my mouth to ask how many people died so that I could save my father, but Miss Rose speaks first. "The agent from Storm and Darkness is responsible for this. Not you. Remember that you helped save your three-dimensional universe from a worse fate."

I close my mouth, not altogether comforted. Even if I did

what she said, I don't think I'll ever forget the unintended consequences of hurling a glass jar at Ty.

We close in on eastern North America and the city of Philadelphia. Miss Rose's fingers insert me through the structure of the Transporter.

"Good luck with your four parents, Jadie. You have the coordinates for the Lowell home and my permission to use the Transporter. Your bracelet, and those belonging to Marius, Ty, and your adoptive parents, are now permanently set in an active state."

"No more pushing me off the Transporter and letting meekers gnaw on my legs?"

"You were never in real danger. I reward those who help me."

Then I plunge ana into the Lowell apartment, landing among a group of agitated people.

"Here she is!"

"Where have you been?"

"What took so long?"

They hug me and turn me around and hug me some more and check me for injuries until I'm dizzy. Only two people stand apart.

One is Ty, who seems to be sulking in a corner.

The other is a tall, thin woman who watches me from

across the room, one hand clasped over her mouth. Her hair is shorter than it was in the photographs, and there are more lines around her eyes.

With trembling hands, I tighten my ponytail and straighten my shirt. "Um. Hi. I'm Jadie."

She lowers her hand. "I always knew you were alive. I never gave up."

I know that voice.

Before I realize I've moved, I'm in her arms and crying—a wet, snotty, *I-can't-catch-my-breath* kind of sobbing, the kind I hate. She holds me, rocking back and forth.

"It's okay, baby. My darling J.D."

✳

My parents tell the Lowells the story of how they were sent to rescue me from the snowbank. Mrs. Lowell asks how the Martins missed the nationwide news coverage of the carjacking and my kidnapping. Mom and Dad wrack their memories and eventually recall a mysterious cable outage in our Kansas neighborhood around the time I arrived in their home. The news blackout must have been arranged so the Martins would never see the story and put two and two together.

I don't know how long the rehashing of my kidnapping would've gone on, but I bring it to a stop when the rumbling inside me can no longer be ignored. "Is there anything to eat?"

Everyone stops their explaining and apologizing and looks at me.

"I missed breakfast. And lunch—and maybe dinner. I don't know what time it is." Then, guiltily, I turn to my birth father. "And, um, you." I don't know what to call him now. "You must've missed more than that."

He has that black cat in his arms, and she's rubbing her head against his chin like she's as happy to have him home as everyone else is. "Dave fed me. But the cuisine was subpar."

My birth mother cups my face with her hands. "I've been waiting *years* to feed you."

All four parents launch into action, and they won't let me help. Marius and Sam are busy gleefully busting Sam's crutch into pieces, so I sit down next to the only miserable person in the apartment.

Mom has bandaged the cut on his back, and he's wearing one of Sam's T-shirts, which hangs to his knees. "I'm surprised you haven't gone home yet," I say. "Marius has the coordinates for your room."

Ty stiffens. "Sorry to intrude on your family reunion. I'll leave."

When he shifts forward to stand up, I elbow him back in place. "That's not what I meant." Because I *do* know why he hasn't gone home. "My dad called your dad and made up a story about an emergency course correction that involved multiple Agents."

"I'm sure my father was pleasant to yours on the phone. Doesn't mean he's going to be pleasant to me."

Feeling sorry for Ty Rivers is an uncomfortable thing. I prefer despising him.

With a sigh, I pick up the viewing crystal from the table where I set it down. No one asked me why I came from 4-space carrying a rock, and now I hand it to Ty. "This is for you."

Ty hefts it. "More mass than it looks like it should have. I assume it's four-dimensional?"

"Yes, and when you're in 4-space, you can see reflections in its facets from *all* directions. It's like looking through a kaleidoscope, but it's better than nothing. Miss Rose gave it to me. You can have it." Ty gives me a funny look, and I scowl. "Don't jump to any wrong conclusions. It doesn't mean I like you."

"It's not *that*," Ty says as if *that* is a stupid idea. "I'm wondering why Miss Rose wants me to have it."

"She gave it to *me*. She didn't know I was going to pass it on to you."

"That's what you think. But what if we've been doing what Miss Rose and the Seers wanted all along? You think finding the Lowells was an accident. But what's the end result? Sam and your father and I create the product they wanted. What if everything that happened was *planned*?"

"Including the part where you helped spies from an enemy clan kidnap my father?"

"Who says they were enemies? What if Dave and Steve were actors? How would we know any different?"

I shake my head. "I wasn't supposed to find the Lowells. Miss Rose tried to scare me away from visiting them."

Ty snorts. "How well did that work? *Were* you scared off?"

For a minute, I consider his point. *You were never in real danger,* Miss Rose said. Did she mean the meeker incident—or the rest of it?

And what about the thousands of Drones crawling over the surface of our braneworld? How come none of them reported Ty's experiments with the Transporter? Was it because I wouldn't have been able to spy on my birth family without his help?

Then I come to my senses. "I know what I saw in 5-space. Miss Rose and Dave weren't acting. They were trying to kill each other."

"What was it like?" Suddenly, Ty's gaze is intense.

What was it like, melding with a being vast enough to be a planet? After that horrible sensation of worms crawling through my flesh and hijacking my body, the link between my mind and SHE felt like stepping into sunlight from out of a dark basement. Seeing in five dimensions . . . using senses I can't explain in a body with parts I have no name for . . . It made me aware that any human individual, including one named Jocelyn Dakota Lowell Martin, is very, very small by comparison.

None of this do I want to share with Ty. They're not secrets. They're . . . personal. But I almost got him eaten, so I owe him *something*.

"You know how humans are like paper dolls in 4-space? Well, in 5-space, we were made of cobwebs. Miss Rose and Dave were like cardboard cutouts, but Dave had an awful lot of insides, which I saw and wish I hadn't. SHE didn't mean to kill him. SHE was just knocking him away from my father, and he went tumbling in a bad direction." I shudder. Reversal in 4-space is a minor inconvenience by comparison. "What 5-space can do to you . . . Let's say that Miss Rose's clan will need a seriously secure port-lock system to prevent accidental *inside-outage* if they plan to colonize there."

Ty stares at me like I haven't given him the answer he wants. Does he expect me to say that being part of SHE was the most exhilarating experience of my life? Because it was and it wasn't. It's something I'll never forget. But I hope it won't be the last amazing thing I do.

Finally, he looks away. "So, Dave wasn't acting when he got killed."

"Or when he was fighting Miss Rose," I agree. "I saw her bleeding."

"That doesn't prove the rest of it wasn't planned by the Seers."

My jaw clenches and my fists curl. Leave it to Ty to complicate what should be an end to the story. But watching him obsessively turn that crystal over and over in his hands, I realize he *needs* the story not to be over.

"Get up," I say.

"What?"

I grab his arm, and he lets me drag him off the sofa. "Get something to eat."

He scowls. "I'm not hungry."

I push him toward the kitchen. "I'd fuel up if I were you. If Miss Rose wants you to have that crystal, you need to figure out why and what she's up to."

Ty narrows his eyes in suspicion. "I thought you didn't believe it."

I *don't* believe everything that happened was a complex plot orchestrated by the Seers, but I understand why Ty Rivers does.

Thanks to today's events, I have double everything: two

mothers, two fathers, two brothers. I don't know how it will work—getting to know the Lowells, adapting to two families—just that it *will*. The details won't matter, and the distance between Kansas and Pennsylvania won't matter, thanks to the Transporter.

Meanwhile, Ty has nothing but conspiracy theories and his evil-genius schemes.

Then again, that's what makes him happy.

So I put on my most serious face and offer my next-door nemesis a gift, just because I can. "You convinced me. Now, go get 'em."

ACKNOWLEDGMENTS

Many years ago when I was in middle school, a teacher handed me the Victorian classic *Flatland* by Edwin Abbott Abbott. (That's not an error; that's really his name.) In *Flatland*, a two-dimensional being, a Square, is visited by a three-dimensional Sphere and introduced to the concept of *up* and *down*, two directions the Square cannot perceive. My favorite part was when the Sphere flipped and reversed a "dog" owned by the Square's daughter, changing it from a mongrel to a pedigree, but my mind was really blown when the Sphere was visited by an Over-Sphere from the fourth dimension!

Years later, when I was an elementary school teacher myself, I discovered the works of YA horror and science fiction author William Sleator. His novel *The Boy Who Reversed Himself* reminded me of my earlier fascination with spatial dimensions and introduced me to the terms *ana* and *kata*. As a salute to the genius of Sleator, I modeled Alia Malik's favorite game, *Cosmic Knight*, on Sleator's *Interstellar Pig*.

In addition to acknowledging the works of Edwin A. Abbott and William Sleator as my inspiration, I want to thank my brilliant agent, Sara Crowe, and my equally brilliant editor, Sally Morgridge, for riding this multidimensional merry-go-round of conspiracy theories and plot twists—and for lending their talents to make this the best book it could be. Thanks also to everyone at Holiday House for their commitment to the project and the beautiful design of the book, inside and out. The ana and kata extensions are stunning, but you'll have to take my word for that, since your three-dimensional eyes aren't built to see them.

Originally titled *Braneworld* and started in 2014, this book has undergone too many versions and drafts to count. I owe a great deal of thanks to my critique partners and beta readers, some of whom have read more than one version over the years. Thank you, Marcy Hatch, Krystalyn Drown, Tiana Smith, Joanne Fritz, Karla Valenti, Julie Dao, Christine Danek, Maria Mainero, Brayden Orpello-McCoy, and Pj McIlvaine.

Finally, I want to express my love and gratitude to my daughters, Gabbey and Gina, for their unwavering support, and to my husband, Bob, for late-night brainstorming sessions in the hot tub under the stars.

"My story is stuck," I said.

"Why not take it to the fifth dimension?" he suggested.